TATER-SKINHEADS

DAVID W. BARBEE

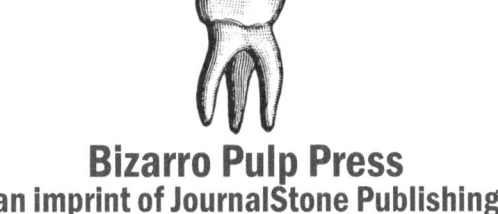

Bizarro Pulp Press
an imprint of JournalStone Publishing

Copyright © 2018 by David W. Barbee

All rights reserved. No part of this book may be used or reproduced by any means, graphic, electronic, or mechanical, including photocopying, recording, taping or by any information storage retrieval system without the written permission of the publisher except in the case of brief quotations embodied in critical articles and reviews.

This is a work of fiction. All of the characters, names, incidents, organizations, and dialogue in this novel are either the products of the author's imagination or are used fictitiously.

Bizarro Pulp Press books may be ordered through booksellers or by contacting:

Bizarro Pulp Press, a JournalStone imprint
    www.BizarroPulpPress.com

The views expressed in this work are solely those of the author and do not necessarily reflect the views of the publisher, and the publisher hereby disclaims any responsibility for them.

    ISBN: 978-1-947654-77-8

Printed in the United States of America
JournalStone rev. date: August 19, 2018

    Cover Art: Justin Coonts

    Interior Formatting: Lori Michelle
        www.theauthorsalley.com

ADVANCE PRAISE FOR TATERSKINHEADS

"Like the drugs in *Taterskinheads*, Barbee's writing hooks you from the very first hit, and you soon find yourself hopelessly addicted."

—Scott Hughes,
author of *The Last Book You'll Ever Read*

"*Taterskinheads* is greasepit noir with a close up view of people being shot in the head, bodies being sliced to ribbons, and faces being flattened with fists."

—Benjamin Anthony

To Sonya, Zelda, and Samson

CHAPTER 1

"**T**HE MIDDLE OF the night is too early for this shit."

Deputy Ramsey wasn't even halfway through her shift when a grungy tweaker showed up at the station's back door and started banging on the glass. She put down her second cup of coffee and poked her head out of the radio room, looking down the corridor to the glass and steel door. It was deadbolted shut at this time of night, but the man on the other side beat his palms against the glass like it would give him sexual release any moment now.

She walked down the hallway and stopped right in front of the glass and crossed her arms. Violet Ramsey was known all over Whaley County as a mean motherfucker with bigger balls than most men. She stood five and a half feet in shimmering black boots, wearing a crisp tan uniform with the department's chocolate brown trim and crimson piping. A thick belt wrapped around her waist, full of black leather pouches and holsters. Her dark hair was gathered at the back of her head in a flat bun.

She approached the back door and squared up to it, eyeing the tweaker glaring at her through the glass with bloodshot eyes. He wore sweatpants and a shirt with a sneering rapper on it, sleeveless to show off his fuzzy black tattoos. Ramsey stood there, saying nothing. The tweaker started slapping the door again. "Let me in!" he shouted. He repeated himself twice more, then stopped when Ramsey took her collapsible baton from her belt and flicked it open at her side.

"What?" she said.

"Let me in! I gotta talk to Willis!"

Willis was Sheriff Ruth's first name, and most everyone called him by it since he was the closest thing Whaley County had to a celebrity. The tweaker was a local, at least. But there was real emotion underneath his manic energy. He was scared.

"Sheriff won't be here till morning," she told him. "Go home and sleep it off."

"No!" he shouted at her, then shrank down at the volume of his own voice. He got closer to the door and said, "Please, I have to talk to him about something. They'll kill me."

Deputy Ramsey's eyebrow arched. "Oh, they'll kill you, will they?"

"If they find out I was here talking to you, yeah. Listen, I'll file a report or somethin', you just gotta make sure Willis reads it. I can't be a part of his shit no more."

"*His* shit?"

"Yeah, bitch, his shit!"

"The sheriff's shit?"

"Naw! Well . . . Actually, it ain't like that no more. This is somethin' new. I've seen it. They keep sayin' the sheriff's down with it but there's no fucking way!"

Ramsey watched the tweaker scratch himself with nervousness. He swatted at the moths that buzzed around the light fixture above. The moths divebombed him and he danced around in circles, swinging his arms and flapping his hands in a dance of energetic stupidity.

This had to be one of the sheriff's guys. Along with knowing his name, everybody knew Willis Ruth ran the county fast and loose. The letter of the law was bureaucratic nonsense, technicalities used to control the country man's life, but Willis Ruth made his name navigating the bullshit. He made the system his bitch and most folks loved him for it. They knew he was extorting Dicky Eastman's car lot. They knew about his connections with the Lieutenant Governor and the local biker mafia. A few of them even knew about the thousands of pounds of methamphetamine that he distributed through Whaley County.

The tweaker here was one of her boss's foot soldiers.

The man outside stopped dancing and remembered why he was there. "Come on! I done told you they're gonna kill me!"

Ramsey took out her keys and shuffled through them. "I'm taking a statement," she said, "then you're back outside."

The man pumped his fist in victory. She unlocked the door and pushed it open. He slipped inside quickly and stood behind her as she locked up again, hopping up and down with excitement.

His enthusiasm made Ramsey uneasy, and since they were all alone, she decided to share her feelings. She spun on her toe and shoved him up against the corridor wall with the point of her elbow pressed deep against his Adam's apple. "Settle the fuck down," she growled at him. "You call me bitch again and you'll regret it. Have respect and you'll get respect, hear?"

He nodded.

Ramsey herded him up the hallway to a small room with a steel table and two chairs. "In here."

The tweaker slipped inside and Ramsey put him in the chair against the wall. She sat closer to the door. On the table in front of her sat a six-year-old laptop covered in dust and coffee splatter. She lifted the lid and booted it up, brought her fingers to the keyboard and typed with quick jabs of her fingers. She opened a new incident report file and looked up at the tweaker. "What's your name?"

He rocked himself back and forth, scanning the corners of the ceiling like he was thinking the question over. He chewed his lip and patted his knees, avoiding eye contact until he finally said, "Naw, you don't need to know that." His eyes cut to her for a split second to gauge her reaction.

"Alright, then," said Deputy Ramsey. "Who's shit are you here to talk about?"

The tweaker leaned in close. "Harv Hallihan," he whispered.

Fuck.

Harv Hallihan lived out in the woods alone, and most people in Whaley County didn't know he existed. But working so close to Sheriff Ruth, Ramsey couldn't help but know a few things about her boss's business partner. Harv had an old farm out by the county line, and it was there that he manufactured all the drugs that the Sheriff trafficked. The rumor was that Harv was some sort of autistic weirdo, smarter than a chemistry professor but couldn't tie his own shoes. Still, he and the Sheriff had been friends since they were boys. Ramsey closed the laptop. "You're an idiot," she said. "And you've come to the wrong place to snitch on Harv."

"No, no, it ain't—"

She leaned over the laptop. "You think we don't know who he is? You think *Willis Ruth* is going to go out and arrest him? For what, exactly?"

"It ain't what you think! It ain't the . . . " He mouthed the word *drugs*. "I know the sheriff and him are pals, man. It's more like . . . Harv's gone rogue, you know?"

"I hate when people say 'you know.' Just tell me what you were going to tell the sheriff. It's not on the record."

He cocked his head and slanted his eyes at her for a few moments. "You're that girl, ain't you? The Marine Girl?"

"Focus, dipshit. This is your last chance."

She saw that fear again, fueling those twitchy eyes. He leaned forward and whispered. "He's making something that's gonna hurt a lot of people. I can't explain it, and I know it sounds nuts. Harv's got smarts, man. All he does is sit over there reading textbooks and shit. He's like an evil scientist, you know? And he's makin' somethin'."

"You mean like a doomsday device?"

The tweaker's eyes lit up. "Exactly! I mean, it's biological, right? But it's basically like a, what you call it, chemical weapon."

Ramsey leaned forward. "What is it?"

"I don't know what it's called! It's somethin' new that Harv fuckin' *invented*! It's crazy, right? An' see, he's makin' it for somebody the Sheriff don't know about. That's the thing. And that motherfucker? I mean, I ain't got a problem with him but he's . . . he's just fuckin' scary. He wants chemical weapons, and he's *serious* about usin' 'em. And he'll kill to keep this shit secret."

Ramsey smiled. She had a pretty smile. Her teeth were nice and straight and to the tweaker it was a scary damn sight. "So tell me the secret, then," she said.

His eyes darted back and forth again. "It's . . . you wouldn't believe me. Just let me explain it to Willis. Please?"

"You haven't even told me your name," she said. "It'll be an anonymous tip."

"Naw," he said, shaking his head. "I know about you. You're the one that ain't in the business. And you don't need to be either, especially not with this shit. I can't, you know, implicate myself. I mean, you'd tell the FBI or something, wouldn't you? Look, all I need is for Willis to straighten this out."

When he finally set his eyes back on Ramsey, her smile had disappeared. "You're fulla shit," she said. "I don't even like taking messages for Sheriff Ruth. You wanna talk to him, come back Monday morning."

"It's Friday night!" he yelled. "I can't go back out there! That scary motherfucker probably knows I'm here, man. He'll fuckin' kill me."

"Then you shouldn't have tried to snitch on him."

"But it's . . . fuckin' important, okay? Just call Willis on your cell phone!"

"You've wasted enough of my time. The bullshit quota's full, so you're leaving now." Ramsey stood up and moved around the table. The tweaker fidgeted in his seat for a few moments, and when she took him by the elbow, he exploded into motion.

His fingers wrapped around her neck and he pushed her back hard. They stumbled around the metal table and nearly tripped, then spun around so fast that the tweaker wound up holding Deputy Ramsey against the wall, pressing his scrawny body with its stinking clothes against her clean uniform. "You think I'm lying, bitch?" he said, his voice turning into a grinding shriek of desperation. "Everything is about to get fucked up and there won't be nothin' left after—"

Ramsey gripped his forearm, stepped between his legs, and with a swift jerk of her hips had him off his feet and spinning end over end. His sneakers hit the ceiling and then his skull crashed onto the tile floor. Laid out flat at her feet, the tweaker let out a dead rabbit sound and rolled over. "Please," he said, and grabbed her boot.

Deputy Ramsey reared back and field goal kicked him in the face. She dragged him down the hallway to the holding cell and locked him in one of the cages. Then she returned to the interview room, booted up the old laptop again, and typed a quick report about an intoxicated suspect who begged for her help and then attacked her when she let him inside, leaving her no option but to retaliate with nonlethal and completely justified force.

"Told you not to call me bitch," she muttered.

✳ ✳ ✳

At seven o'clock the sun rose over the pines. Ramsey was on her fourth cup of coffee when she heard the back door unlock. She finished off the cup and grabbed her duffel bag from under the desk, then made her way out into the hallway to see Deputy Duane Maxwell walking in. Maxwell was tall and skinny, with knobby shoulders and a pinched-up face.

He worked with Sheriff Ruth on the day shift. His mother was also the sheriff's stepsister, and he could never manage to refrain from calling his boss Uncle Willis. It was an open secret that Maxwell was being groomed to replace the sheriff one day.

Deputy Maxwell stopped in front of the holding room and peeked his head inside. "Who's that?" he said, pointing to the unconscious tweaker inside one of the cages.

Ramsey approached with her duffel bag over her shoulder. She stopped and looked in at the prisoner. "Didn't say," she said. "He was high. Wanted to talk to the boss. I wrote it up."

"Probably about—well, never mind."

"Yeah," Ramsey said, "I don't need to hear it. You know, for the day when we're all taken to court."

Maxwell winked at her. "Won't ever happen, babe." Ramsey's stomach turned. She moved for the back door.

"Hey!" Maxwell called after her. "Looks like he's got a shiner . . . up the side of his face."

"He was impolite," she said as she exited.

Maxwell giggled. "Oh, shit."

CHAPTER 2

WHALEY COUNTY BOILED down to a loose knot of highways carved through the scrubby pines, stocked with plenty of churches and truck stops, but only two strip malls. It was a stereotype of the middle of nowhere, but Violet Ramsey liked living in the middle of nowhere. There was peace and quiet in the obscurity, even as the whole world spun around it.

Ramsey drove an old Chevy Blazer, glittery black once upon a time. Now the roof and hood were scorched dull by a couple decades in the sun. She drove thirty minutes across the county to get to her place. Her street, only recently paved, split off from the highway and trailed through some cow fields to her family's old doublewide trailer on a three-acre plot. Since her mother left, Ramsey had turned the house into her personal sanctuary.

The closest neighbor lived a few lots back up the street, past three foreclosed trailers sitting in waist-high grass. The seclusion was important to Ramsey because she was technically famous. Everyone in Whaley County knew about her, because even before she became the so-called Marine Girl, she had started out as the girl with the dead father.

Lance Corporal Martin Ramsey blew his head off

in his truck when his only child was just sixteen. There was no suicide note, and no explanation. Already a quiet, bookish girl, the death of her father drew young Violet deeper into herself. This only heightened the scrutiny, with teachers and doctors and her own mother seeing nothing but red flags. She escaped the glare on her eighteenth birthday when she joined the Corps.

Her mother cried as her baby was shipped off to Parris Island to live amongst the roughnecks. Even then, Violet could admit that she was running away. Running away from pain, loss, and the sheer terror of what her father had done to himself. But she was also running toward something. Something that became her whole world. Just like her father, she made for an excellent Marine. Everything she was told, she memorized. Everything they asked, she did. Finally, she could be seen for what she could do, not things that had happened to her. For the first time in her life she didn't feel like a victim. The glare of fame took a new form. Ramsey's instructors praised her focus, her intensity, her presence of mind. They said she shot like Annie Oakley and ran every obstacle course like "a chimpanzee fucking a cheetah, a true thing of beauty." It was the sort of fame Ramsey could get used to. This spotlight was powered by respect.

By the time she earned her globe, anchor, and eagle, Violet Ramsey was near the top of her class and the best female recruit on the base. At graduation she actually cried when she hugged her mother. It was a big, nourishing slice of the American dream, just for her. In a week's time they shipped her off to Iraq, and with her credentials, she was thrown right into the grinder.

She spent a whole six days in the theater before she was hurt and sent home. They refused to give details, just told Violet's mother that she'd survived a lethal engagement during a classified exercise. Violet rolled off the plane in a wheelchair, one leg broken, the other sprained, ribs cracked and all the teeth knocked out of her head. Her mother drove her back home, just happy that her baby was alive.

During the recovery, nestled back in her hometown, Ramsey saw her notoriety mutate into something far worse than pity. She became the Marine Girl, respected and admired, treated like a hero by people who hadn't seen the bullets and bombs and dead people. Her short-lived career in the Corps had turned into another meal for her small town to feed upon. They went back to gawking at her, this time with admiration, which somehow made it worse.

Ramsey pulled into her gravel driveway and climbed out of the Blazer. She walked up the porch steps to her trailer and unlocked the front door, which was made from oak and set within a steel frame she'd bolted in herself. She went inside and locked the door behind her, then let out a long, slow breath. She dropped her duffel bag on the short table in the front room and executed her private routine in just four minutes.

She took off her belt and her badge and put them in a drawer in the kitchen. Then she went to the dinner table and sat down to unlace and remove her giant black boots. Then she went to the bedroom, removed her uniform, and hung the shirt and slacks on wire hangers, filing them away in the closet with six other pairs. In her t-shirt and underwear, like she was back in the barracks, Ramsey went to her bedside table and sat down. In the drawer was her stash. She packed a bowl with sharp granules of crystal meth, then removed her dentures and clenched the skinny glass stem between her hardened gums. Her movements were fluid and quick, heavily practiced. She lit the end of the pipe with a three-inch flame from a cigarette lighter and sucked the noxious smoke deep into her lungs.

Ramsey walked out of the bedroom with a gentle glide instead of her usual march, a trail of acrid smoke following her. When her casts came off, Ramsey tried all sorts of drugs to ease her post-traumatic stress. At first she felt like she was following in her father's footsteps; yet another soldier driven crazy and on the fast track to self-termination. Thankfully, she ran into an old classmate who was cool enough to sell her street drugs, and strangely enough, it was methamphetamines that calmed her down. Ramsey never imagined herself as a tweaker, but damned if crank didn't take the edge off. It kept her relaxed, which made it possible to do her job, which made it possible to pay her bills, buy more crank, and just keep existing. She smoked an ounce of the stuff every week in her secluded doublewide paradise.

Ramsey dropped onto the couch and switched on her flatscreen TV, which was so big it seemed to take up most of the living room wall. She flipped through a hundred satellite channels while she smoked, never staying put for more than a few seconds. When the pipe was cashed she got up, warm electricity buzzing all through her. Scooby Doo filled the gigantic screen.

She put on some shorts and went outside. The backyard was a scrubby mess, but in the center of it, in front of the porch, was a raised garden built it in the shape of an 'X.' Ramsey kept it filled with a careful blend of soils and fertilizers. She grew peppers mostly, a few different flower strains, even some herbs and berries. When she first came home, Ramsey's mother took her on a few trips to the VFW hall in the next county. They had lots of advice that Ramsey politely dismissed until she finally told her mother stop taking her there, but they were the ones who told her about constructive activities like gardening, and over time Ramsey had to admit that the old vets had been right. Constructive activity was fun and healthy, and digging out weeds while stoned to the gills felt fucking wonderful.

Noon came and went. Ramsey worked in the garden until the rush of energy faded away. Sweaty and sleepy, she washed her hands and climbed into bed and slept, heavy curtains blocking the daylight outside.

CHAPTER 3

SHE WOKE UP after just four hours of sleep and went for her pipe, packed it and smoked it down to nothing.

The sun was still shining. It was the weekend.

The first thing to do was stock her provisions. Ramsey took a shower and dressed in layers despite the heat, pulling a cap onto her head. She shopped at the Food Lion at the center of the county. It was one of the few places she visited outside of work, and she prided herself on getting in and out quickly. Ramsey pushed the wire cart at a brisk pace and avoided eye contact with anyone who passed her in the aisles. She threw in some canned goods, mostly vegetable soup, and a small mountain of chocolate pudding packs. She knew exactly how much it took to feed herself for seven days.

With the groceries loaded up in the Blazer, Ramsey sat back in the driver's seat and let herself relax for a few minutes. She looked across the parking lot at the dusty cars and watched the people meandering in and out of the store before a baby blue Escalade caught her eye. Ramsey watched the hulking machine glide into a tight parking spot near the front of the store. A skinny woman in a silk blouse climbed out of the Escalade, along with four young girls, a boy, and bringing up the rear was Doug Crosby.

In all of Whaley County, Doug Crosby probably knew Ramsey the best. It wasn't saying much, only that they were in the same grade in school and enlisted at the same time. They were recruits together at Parris Island. He saw firsthand her metamorphosis into the Marine Girl, but he didn't follow her overseas. At the end of basic training, Doug was shifted into military intelligence, then he eventually dropped out, earned his law degree, and moved back to home to marry his high school sweetheart and open a practice. It was Doug who told everybody about Ramsey the badass soldier. The warrior. The American hero. He was to blame for her current reputation. She watched Doug cross the parking lot, following his herd into the Food Lion, his head buried in his phone. She thought about running him over, but instead she drove home.

Ramsey moved her groceries inside and then stacked them up in the cupboard while smoking another bowl. She smoked the rest of the day and all through the night. Sunday morning came and she'd been awake for forty hours, wired, alert, and ready for the weekly phone call from her mother.

When she was growing up they barely got along. Violet took after her father, a lone wolf instead of a social butterfly, and when he died the two of them nearly became strangers. Violet's mother found a new man, too quickly in Violet's judgment, but before long she was in the Corps and didn't have to watch them make out on her father's couch.

When Violet returned from Iraq, broken down physically and mentally, her mother suddenly reset herself. She didn't ask about life in the military or the details of Violet's engagement. To her thinking, it was enough that her daughter was alive and didn't have to go back. Whatever horror she'd endured could be thanked at least for that, and she rededicated herself to caring for her daughter. Violet opened up enough to assure her mother that she was okay, or at least okay enough that she'd never kill herself. Not after enduring her own father's suicide. That was music to her mother's ears. She took care of Violet until she could literally stand on her own legs again. Ramsey then insisted that she could take care of herself, and her mother, satisfied that the hard times were over, remarried and moved to the city. She signed the doublewide over to Violet, but made sure to call every Sunday morning before church. She wanted their relationship to stay strong, and it worked best with rituals that allowed them to be in each other's lives and out of each other's hair.

Ramsey sat on the couch and took out her cell phone. Her mother answered her call the way she always did. "Hey, Girlfriend."

"Hey, Mom."

"How are things?"

"Good. Everything's the same over here. The roof's leaking in the guest bedroom's closet. I gotta get up there and fix it."

"Just hire a guy. You can afford it."

"I can fix it is what I can do."

"Well just be careful."

"Gotcha."

"I know you like to keep busy, like when you painted all the walls black. I still can't believe you did that."

Ramsey remembered that weekend fondly, forty

hours of painting while high off her ass. She painted four coats of it in every room. They were all black as pitch now. Her mother always said she couldn't believe that Ramsey did that.

"How's Terrence?"

Her mother laughed. "Still going on about some civil war between the members at his golf course. I've stopped paying attention to it."

During these talks Violet imagined her mother fixing her makeup and trying on jewelry. She listened to her talk about the things she'd done that week. She listened to her talk about how little she listened to Terrence. Soon enough it was time for church, a deadline that made these conversations just the right length. They both said, "I love you," and hung up.

Ramsey took out her teeth and got high for the rest of the morning. She lay on the floor of the living room, eyes barely open, mumbling through her gums, dreaming.

✸ ✸ ✸

At sunset it was time to start the next ritual: cleaning herself up. These rituals she'd developed allowed her to have an outwardly legitimate life while constantly filling her body with illicit and very toxic drugs. Ramsey felt no shame in being a drug addict, but she felt the title came with extra responsibility. She had to take care of herself, especially after these weekend benders where she had barely slept.

It took the last twenty-four hours of her weekend to do properly, so she didn't look like any other hollow-eyed sore-ridden psychopath out on the street. First she did some exercises on the living room floor, working up a sweat and burning off as much energy as she could. It never tired her out, and she knew to stop after three hours before her head started to spin. Then she went to the trailer's master bathroom and rinsed her face and hair in the sink, clearing away the sweat.

The evening pressed on and Ramsey forced herself to drink some soup by midnight. Another rule of hers was to eat five times a week. The fact that she was hardly ever hungry made the rule imperative. She watched TV into the dark of night while she sipped her soup, chewing individually on each little tasteless vegetable.

She finished eating as the sun came up and hit the pipe once more to take the edge off. Then she took a long cold shower, slowly shampooing her hair. After that she needed to get a few hours of sleep, which meant taking a fistful of painkillers.

Six hours later she staggered awake, her eyes snapping open and her mind suddenly alert. She got up on numb legs, stumbling like a newborn foal, and drew a hot bath. Ramsey gently scrubbed her skin with a sponge, her movements slow and meticulous. Halfway through the bath she felt like smoking again but pushed the craving aside. This was part of the process, too, because she'd learned that if she bathed while high she'd lose track of time and wind up scouring her skin off for a few hours.

Ramsey washed her face with several brands of moisturizer and when she got out of the tub she applied a facial mask. The tacky green gunk on her face almost made her look feminine. She took out her dentures and gave the mirror a crooked grin. She looked like the Wicked Witch of the West.

She brushed her dentures. She washed her hair

again. She smoked a few more bowls over the afternoon, peeled the green gunk off her face, and donned a freshly ironed uniform. By the time the evening rolled around, Violet Ramsey smelled like a new car and her face was as smooth as glass.

CHAPTER 4

SHE WALKED INTO work twenty minutes early. After locking the back door behind her, she turned to see Deputy LaGrange posted up against the wall.

Lenny LaGrange was a smug boy in a barrel-chested man's body. He once played football at Auburn but washed out of the program halfway through his sophomore year. After that he'd been run off from every job he got until he came across Sheriff Ruth, who saw a young meathead ready to be molded into his own personal pit bull. LaGrange spent most of his shifts riding around collecting the sheriff's dues, but on a busy evening he got to rap a few knuckles and break some heads. He'd never shot anyone but he spent a lot of time imagining and describing scenarios where he'd get the chance. These were everyday scenes—someone shouts at him, walks toward him, looks at him—but they had yet to materialize.

Sometimes LaGrange worried that he'd never get to respond with legally justified murder. Nobody in Whaley County would dream of fucking with one of Willis Ruth's deputies. There was peace these days. The sheriff hadn't even ordered LaGrange to pistol whip a man in months, and while that fact frustrated LaGrange to no end, not even he was stupid enough to disobey. He was a man of immense frustration, and he often took it out on Ramsey. LaGrange strolled up to her, chewing on a toothpick. "The boss wants to see you," he said.

"What's he want?" she asked.

"To *see* you, dumbass."

Ramsey shouldered past him and headed for Sheriff Ruth's office at the end of the hall. LaGrange trotted up behind her.

"Hey, that tweaker you brought in from the other night? He up and died on us."

Ramsey's heart dropped but she kept walking, eyes forward.

"You was the last one to see him alive," LaGrange said. "I'd be shittin' my pants if I was you. It's been a long Monday and Sheriff's still here. He don't do that unless there's an ass to be chewed."

Ramsey stopped outside Sheriff Ruth's door with LaGrange's face hovering right over her shoulder. She turned her head and eyeballed him. "Fuck off, Lenny. Right now." LaGrange threw up his hands in mock surrender and backed away, chuckling to himself.

Ramsey put her duffel bag on the floor outside the doorway and walked in. Sheriff Ruth sat behind his desk, looking down at a spread of papers. She knocked on the door to get his attention but the sheriff didn't look up. "You wanted to see me, sir?" she said, standing at attention. He motioned to the chair in front of his desk. Ramsey sat down and didn't move a muscle. There was no way the sheriff was pissed at her.

Unless he was.

Sheriff Willis Ruth was tall and rakish, with bright silver hair that looked blue in certain lights. His face was tanned dark and he had a mustache of pure black. He'd been just as handsome back in high school. Willis Ruth was too skinny to play football but still dated all the cheerleaders. He could beat any of his peers in a fistfight or a drag race, and he could laugh just like Burt Reynolds. He got deputized practically right out of high school, and like Ramsey, he'd become famous.

It was when Danny Boy Buckley came through town three decades ago. Deputy Ruth stopped the upcoming country music star's tour bus when it hopped a curb and bent a stop sign over. Danny Boy was a legend on the festival circuit and was in no mood to be hassled by a youngster with a badge, so while Deputy Ruth spoke with the bus driver and two bodyguards about the bent over stop sign, Danny Boy came out and commenced to cursing his name and threatening to whoop his ass. He put his finger in young Willis Ruth's face and told him he was in deep shit. The deputy cold-cocked him in the jaw, then fought off the two bodyguards and arrested everybody on the tour bus.

Whaley County elected him sheriff the next year, and Sheriff Ruth's standing in the community had only grown since then. He'd served longer than anybody on the county board and almost everyone up at the courthouse. Most importantly, he knew how to handle his fame. He kept the citizens happy and ran his department like a family business, prizing loyalty above all else. He paid his deputies like soldiers for hire and he drove a late model Charger painted Dukes of Hazzard orange. Covering the walls of his office wall were plaques in the shape of the county or state. Behind him sat a large gun safe, a shelf full of model hotrods, and an expensive new computer. He'd never married or had children, though he still dated cheerleaders in his spare time.

Sheriff Ruth stared down at his papers through thick reading glasses. He believed in keeping immaculate records, especially since so much of what his department did was off the books. After an extremely long silence, he finally said, "Have a good weekend?"

"I did," said Ramsey.

Ramsey had to be careful around the sheriff. He not only had a sharp talent for talking to people, he was also a good listener. He could sniff out any lie a man told, but Ramsey had her reputation on her side. She was a strict and dutiful deputy. Everyone believed she was just Marine Girl, the robotic badass. When she took the job she told Sheriff Ruth that all she wanted was to be a cog in the machine. For the most part, this was actually the truth. She didn't care about his illegal activities and was willing to be a part of his corrupt team as long as she was mostly left alone. Still, she could never risk Willis Ruth figuring out her lies. Let him think she was a robot. He might be slick but he was still just a man, and men always underestimated women.

Sheriff Ruth looked up from his papers. "I need to know about Friday night," he said bluntly. "I read the report you filed."

"It's all in there," she said.

"He said he wanted to talk to me?"

"Yes, sir."

"Why?"

"Didn't say."

"Why did you let him inside?"

"He said somebody was going to kill him."

"Who?"

"Didn't say." The sheriff stopped his rapid-fire questions to glare over the desk at her with his bright blue eyes. Ramsey met his gaze. "I gave him a few minutes to explain," she said. "I told him what I'd do to him if he freaked out. He freaked out anyway."

Sheriff Ruth's black eyebrows bobbed at her. "He didn't say who was going to kill him?" he offered.

"No, sir."

"Didn't say anything about me?"

Once again, with complete clarity, she said, "No, sir."

Sheriff Ruth finally looked away. He leaned back in his chair and clucked his tongue. Ramsey blinked. "He wasn't making sense, sir," she said. "Most of it was gibberish. I tried to get some details but he was fried up. Could be his dealer was after him. Could be his own mother for all I know. But when he put his hands on me I had to stomp him."

The sheriff's nodded up at the ceiling tiles. "Well, that's understandable."

"Did he say anything?" she asked. "Or did he just . . . ?"

Sheriff Ruth cut his eyes at her for a moment, sizing up her curiosity. "Fella just sputtered out and died," he said. "Won't know the cause until the coroner gets back to me about it. I think you might've concussed him."

"I'm . . . sorry."

"Naw, don't worry about it. He was a drug addict. When you're dealin' with those sorts it's bound to happen."

"I know police brutality is a serious thing. I wouldn't want . . . "

"I said relax. Nothing's gonna come of it."

"Thank you, sir."

"Alright, then. Get on your shift."

He was annoyed with her now. Excellent. Back to normal. Ramsey went to the dispatcher's desk in the station's lobby. She set down her things, as she always did, and listened for Sheriff Ruth and LaGrange. Soon she heard their voices in the hallway, then they walked out the back door together.

She waited ten minutes and then went to the interview room. She started up the laptop, checked the report she'd filed, and saw that a new paragraph had been added. The report now identified the tweaker as Rubin Music. He woke up at noon on Friday, said some garbled words to Deputy Maxwell, and then fell face first to the floor. Maxwell called in an ambulance and Music was pronounced dead on arrival. The paragraph was written well, which meant it was Sheriff Ruth's work.

And it wasn't the whole story, either. The important part was that they didn't know anything Rubin Music had told her, and that was all Ramsey really cared about. The only part that bothered her was Sheriff Ruth drilling her for info even after he'd finished the official report. He had to know that Music worked for Harv Hallihan, but he still didn't know the so-called evil shit Harv was up to. Something was rotten in Willis' business, and he'd be on the scent soon enough.

For some reason, that bothered Ramsey more than the fact that she'd kicked a man to death.

CHAPTER 5

SHE LOOKED UP Rubin Music on her computer at home.

He was twenty-one with no high school diploma, no work history, and four arrests for sale of a controlled substance, each time in neighboring Tyrell County, near the city. That made him one of Harv's pushers.

Ramsey lit up her pipe and stared at the screen. She wondered why she even cared. The safe thing to do was let Sheriff Ruth deal with it. It was his business, and she'd still have her job no matter how it shook out. Ramsey sucked on her pipe as her thoughts began to spin. She leaned back in her chair and closed her eyes and fell into a buzzing vortex.

For the moment, she knew something the sheriff didn't. That was a rare thing. Eventually, he'd catch up to Harv's little scheme and likely put a stop to it. But in the meantime . . .

This could be an opportunity.

Ramsey had time to make a move.

What kind of move?

Ramsey's thoughts zeroed in on Harv Hallihan like a blood-red laser beam. She had to get to him before Sheriff Ruth. There was no trace of him on the internet, but it was a small community and she knew a few things. The Hallihan property was a fifty-acre tract of land that they'd farmed for generations until Harv came along. Supposedly, he was smart as hell, and even earned a scholarship to some ivy league University, but he never finished. His parents, living alone on the giant farm, fell sick and he returned home to care for them. The farm fell into disrepair and they passed, leaving Harv as the last of his kin. At some point after that, he was approached by Sheriff Ruth and brought on board to cook meth. With Harv's scientific mind and Sheriff Ruth's charismatic leadership, they manufactured and sold hundreds of pounds of product. They used some of Willis' other connections to ship the stuff all across the southeast, and so far no one had traced it back to Whaley County.

They'd had a good business going for years now, but for some reason Harv was making his own moves behind Willis' back.

That made Harv vulnerable.

Ramsey looked up his property records and found the tax information for his fifty acres. One of those acres was zoned for commercial use. It was a little square that jutted out and connected his land to a highway. Ramsey looked up the address and found the name White Star Shooting Range. There was no advertising for the place anywhere on the net. It had to be a front to launder Harv's drug money.

The old fucker had to be sitting on a fortune in cold, untraceable cash.

Ramsey took a long drag on her pipe.

She could take out Harv. She'd be doing everyone a favor.

The sheriff. Maybe he wouldn't care that Harv was dead.

But maybe he would. Harv was his partner.

Maybe he'd be so pissed that he'd sniff her out finally. She wouldn't just lose her job. He'd bust her. For everything.

Wait.

Fuck the job.

If she did this right the job wouldn't matter. Ramsey could get Harv's cash, dump his body, and disappear from Whaley County long before anyone figured her out. Eventually they would suspect her, but by then they'd never find her.

It was a lot to digest.

She hit the pipe again and giggled under her breath. She'd just laid out a plan to murder a man and steal his stash of drug money. Ramsey was as risk-averse as they come, but she could see the pathway to this perfect crime so clearly it made her itch.

It'd be easy.

So why not?

CHAPTER 6

IT FELT GOOD to have a mission again. Ramsey sobered up a little and hit the road while it was still morning. She rarely ventured out on a weekday, yet there she was in the summer heat on a hastily hatched plan to kill a man.

The first task was reconnaissance. She needed to see who she was dealing with, because it wouldn't just be Harv. There were worker bees like Rubin Music, running Harv's errands or possibly protecting him, and she was willing to bet they worked at that White Star Shooting Range. She had to scope these workers out before putting the hit on their boss. If there was an army of shitkickers at the range, then this mission of hers was drug-induced nonsense.

But if it was a skeleton crew, she was good to go.

GPS led her out to the eastern edge of the county, where the road signs were half-swallowed by thick swaths of kudzu that crept out into the road. The range was located around a wide bend in the highway. It was marked with a plywood sign that was painted black with a bullet hole drawn in the center dripping drops of red blood. *White Star Shooting Range* framed the bloody hole. Ramsey pulled into the gravel driveway and parked her Blazer in front of a square steel building.

Ramsey took a deep breath. She got out of the Blazer, hooking her duffel bag over a shoulder, and marched for the door. She passed a muddy pickup with a gun rack and a beige F350 with chrome trim. She knew she should stop and take down the license plate numbers, but the camera mounted over the building's front door was already watching her. She walked up to the door without hesitation and opened it.

Inside, Ramsey found herself at the end of a hallway heading along the front wall. The walls and ceiling were unpainted particleboard, patched with posters and bumper stickers with politicians' names and slogans she didn't bother reading. She followed the hall to a corner of the warehouse, where it turned and deposited her into a saloon from an old movie. The walls were yellow pine planks, burnished and lacquered. At the top of each wall were rows of mounted deer heads. She expected shelves and racks full of weapons, but there was only a pegboard behind a bar, covered with a few rifles and shotguns.

She heard gunshots, though. Beyond another door in the saloon area was the shooting range, crackling with automatic fire.

Ramsey walked up to the bar. Two men sat at the corner on the end, playing cards. The first one was short and redheaded, with a square face like a brick with freckles. The other was scrawny and tattooed, with greasy hair that hung over the shaved sides of his head. Both of them wore black t-shirts.

The greasy guy looked up at Ramsey as she approached. "I need to do some shooting," she said, making her voice pleasant and feminine, like her mother's. "Where do I sign up?"

He smirked and turned back to his cards. "You don't sign up. The shooting gallery is through there. Have at it."

Another repetitive roar of gunfire sounded off. "Thank you," she chirped.

The redheaded one spoke up right before she passed through the doorway. "You're that Marine Girl, aren't you?"

Ramsey turned. His voice had the same gentle and feminine tone that she had used, but his eyes glared at her like a bird of prey.

She stared back for a second. "Yeah."

The bird of prey eyes didn't blink. "Thank you for your service," he said. The greasy guy chuckled and they both turned their attention back to the cards.

Ramsey walked through the saloon door and was met with a chain link fence that went all the way to the ceiling. A line of wooden stalls had been built against it. Beyond the fence was the majority of the warehouse's space, a bare concrete floor with tall stacks of sandbags and plywood at the opposite wall. Each stack had targets set up to match one of the stalls.

Ramsey went to a stall and put her duffel bag on the little table inside. There wasn't much to this range. It felt like little more than a clubhouse for these guys. Her reservations about knocking over Harv were fading fast.

She put in her earplugs just as another blast of automatic fire sounded. She looked up into the gallery and saw a ribbon of red-hot bullets zigzagging across several of the targets. Even with her earplugs in, the thunderous rattle of it filled the warehouse and echoed off the metal walls. Ramsey opened her bag and picked up her Glock. She fired off a shot and a tiny spot of plywood next to the target burst into splinters.

She thought about the plan as she squeezed the trigger every other second, settling into a robotic rhythm. Killing Harv wouldn't be difficult. The real trick would be finding his hoard of cash. She might have to torture it out of him. The only one protecting Harv was Sheriff Ruth, and he had no stroke outside the county. He'd never find her after the deed was done. As for her mother . . . they functioned separately enough that Ramsey was comfortable severing that string. The only real problem was Harv's new partner, the one Rubin was so nervous about. The so-called scary motherfucker.

Maybe he was the one shooting the assault rifle.

The Glock clicked empty. Ramsey opened the slide, held the gun up to her face, and blew a stream of air through the barrel. It whistled in the silence. She put the gun away and slung her duffel bag over her shoulder.

When she turned to leave the stall, she found a man standing by the doorway to the saloon. He had an AR15 strapped to his chest, his hands draped over it like a dog's paws. He was a grizzled man in his fifties, wearing clean Nikes and jean shorts and a canary yellow polo shirt. Dark aviator sunglasses hid his eyes. He was clearly a dad, and his thinning red hair made her guess that the brick-faced boy in the saloon was his.

"You shoot pretty well," he said to her. He then turned his back to her and walked back down the lane to his stall.

Ramsey went into the saloon and walked up to the two guys playing cards. She pointed a thumb back to the shooting gallery. "Is that guy the manager?"

"You got a complaint?" said the greasy one, not looking up from his cards.

Ramsey couldn't suppress a grin. She shook it off and raised a defensive hand. "I'm sorry. I just haven't heard an AR in a few years."

The redhead looked up at her and said, "Do you have post-traumatic stress? I bet you do."

"I don't think I was there long enough to get it," she said.

"But you saw some shit, right?" said the greasy guy. "How many hajis did you kill?"

They both looked up at her, waiting to see her reaction.

"None," she said.

The redhead spoke up. "Are you here on official business? We'd like to know why you're here. Is there some kind of problem?"

Ramsey reached into her pocket and produced her wallet. She took out a stack of hundred dollar bills. "I'm tired of shooting at trees in my backyard," she said. "I needed a little change of scenery for my practice, that's all. Plus I was thinking about buying that thirty-ought on the wall there. But now..." Ramsey moved to a little wire shelf on another wall, stocked with tactical gear and boxes of bullets. She picked up a black cardboard box with neon green words on it. "Now I'm just gonna buy these night vision goggles."

CHAPTER 7

RAMSEY CAME INTO the station that night like she always did and waited an hour after LaGrange drove away to make her move.

She unplugged the phone, locked up the station behind her, and jogged out to her Blazer. She'd bailed on work before. Six times over nine years, each instance used to rush home and get high, an indulgence. She wasn't proud of it, and she knew that each time could have easily ruined her. But this time was to commit a few felonies, score a fortune in drug money, and then disappear forever. If everything went as planned then she would return to the station as if nothing had happened, and after her shift was through, she'd be home free.

She took the highway out toward the White Star Shooting Range and drove a quarter mile past it. Farther down was a dove field in the trees on Harv's property line. She shut off the Blazer's headlights and drove onto the field. She parked by the trees, hidden in darkness, and hopped out.

She quickly removed her uniform and put on black fatigues. She put a different pair of boots that were so old they would only leave plain, flat footprints. She slung a small black satchel over her back and cinched the cord tight. A black ski mask went over her head and the night vision goggles were strapped on over that. She clicked the power button and a bright green display lit up the inside of the goggles. She brought them down over her eyes and locked up the Blazer.

Ramsey could always hike at a good pace, even in the dark. The woods were thick but the goggles helped. She could see a hundred yards before everything became a dark green blur. There was no way to know where Harv's actual residence was, just that it was on the Tyrell County side. That left her with around fifty acres. She sized it up in her mind and steered herself up the middle of the property, running through towering pines and ducking under ropes of briars.

It took two hours to find a dirt road, far longer than Ramsey would've liked. She stopped in the road and took a knee, her lungs pulsing in her chest. She removed the goggles and took ten deep breaths. It was two in the morning and she promised herself she'd be back at the station by sunrise.

The road wound through the trees, heading east and west. Harv's place could be in either direction. Ramsey picked one and started running again. The trail turned back and forth through the trees, but the goggles had a compass built into the display. It helped her keep her bearings so she didn't worry that she was getting herself lost.

Within ten minutes the road led to an opening. Spread out before her were several acres worth of fields. The ones closest to her were flat, but the other half were overgrown with weeds and anthills. Separating them was an old oak tree, and several dark buildings. There was a giant barn, a cabin missing half its roof, and a little singlewide trailer with a light in its window.

Ramsey circled around to approach from the overgrown fields, keeping low behind grasses and saplings. She hopped a fence of sagging barbed wire and ran up behind the dilapidated cabin. Ramsey flattened herself against the soft wood and followed it around the corner. From there she darted to the oak tree, which felt brittle and dead when she touched it. Harv's whole place felt ancient and petrified, like ruins from the past.

From beneath the tree she had a good view of the trailer. It still sat on its wheels, with nothing blocking the crawlspace, so Ramsey darted through the knee-high grass and dove underneath. She crawled ten feet over to the window with the light. She removed her goggles and listened . She heard typing, and a voice. Ramsey moved out from under the trailer and stretched upward to the window's dusty screen. She peeked over the edge and looked inside.

The inside of the trailer was almost empty. The drywall was still white and the carpet clean. The kitchen was bare except for twenty boxes of Cheerios lined up neatly on the counter. The living room just beyond had a few dozen textbooks on the floor lined up along the length of the wall. In the center of the room was a small table with a computer and for a monitor there was a flatscreen television mounted to the wall. Sitting at the table was Harv Hallihan.

Harv was small, wearing an ironed-stiff shirt and slacks. He sat in a simple kitchen chair with very good posture. His hair was dark gray and combed, though it looked like he cut it himself. He looked every bit the scientist, tapping away on his keyboard. Ramsey tried to see what he was typing. What looked like computer code scrolled up the screen, like some sort of mathematical diagram. As he typed, he spoke into a Bluetooth. Harv's voice was a deep, even drone. Ramsey listened.

"I don't believe you, Willis. You're accusing me of somethin' here. Fact is, your department killed one of my employees. Murdered him. Now I'm a man short and my whole system's fucked up. He was the one brought my groceries, Willis."

He stopped talking for a minute.

"Don't deny it, Willis. He died in your jail. Now, I don't know what he told you, but you should realize that that boy was out of his head pretty much all the time. We ain't dealing with the brightest bulbs here, but that's no excuse to kill him." He paused again before saying one last thing.

"Leave me be, Willis. I don't need you hanging over my shoulder hen-pecking me. I have everything under control. *You're* the fuck up here, not me." He ended the phone call and switched off the flatscreen. In the screen's black reflection, Ramsey saw her forehead at the bottom corner of the window. She ducked down immediately as Harv stood up from the table.

Ramsey hid beneath the trailer again and listened to Harv's footsteps move across the room. She brought her satchel around and slowly opened it. She took out her Glock and put the goggles back on.

A light bulb over the front door came alive and nearly blinded her. The door opened and Harv stepped out onto the porch. He descended the steps and headed off into the grass, walking casually as the stalks slapped at his legs. He headed toward a barn that loomed over the flat, moonlit fields.

Ramsey moved out from beneath the trailer. She crept through the grass after Harv. Through the night vision goggles he was a bright green cartoon of a man, a glowing animation separate from her reality. She moved faster, closing in on him. Ramsey raised her gun, ready to bash in the back of his skull and take him prisoner, to make him give up everything he had before she wiped him out like the blobby green smudge he was.

Harv stopped suddenly, and in half a moment he heard the grass rustling behind him. He turned to see a black-clad ninja standing in the grass a few feet away, backlit by the light bulb on his porch. Ramsey stopped as the shining white orbs of Harv Hallihan's eyes saw her and her gun.

She hesitated. It felt like hours, but it was just long enough for Harv to turn back around and make a break for the barn.

He was fast for a man his age, and he didn't seem to think she'd shoot him in the back. He was right, she needed him alive.

"Fuck!" she growled, and started after him.

Harv disappeared into the open barn door and a light switched on. Ramsey got halfway there before Harv reemerged holding a shotgun. Ramsey turned on a dime and ran around the structure as Harv blasted a slug after her.

Ramsey moved alongside the barn and heard him rack another cartridge behind her. She turned a corner on the other side of the barn and then bolted into the open field. Her boots sank into freshly plowed dirt and slowed her down. She pushed herself, making long strides with every ounce of energy she had, but the harder she pushed herself the more she realized that this mission was the stupidest thing she'd ever done. Harv was taking aim behind her. She was going to be shot in the back and die in this field.

But there was no shotgun blast. Instead she heard Harv yelling to her.

"No!" he called.

Ramsey stole a glance behind her and saw him at the edge of the dirt, the shotgun lying on the ground next to him. She slowed down to a jog, still looking over her shoulder. "Stop!" Harv yelled, waving his arms like a maniac. Ramsey came to a stop and crouched, drawing her weapon. She took aim. There was still time to kill him and unfuck the situation. Ramsey lined him up in her sights, but something stopped her. A sound, high pitched and guttural.

Harv began crawling into the field, using his hands to tidy up the rows of dirt where she'd disturbed them. Like he was trying to cover her tracks for her. The guttural whine grew louder and Harv worked faster, piling up little mounds of soil and crawling forward for more. Ramsey lowered her weapon and looked at the footsteps she had left through the dirt. Around each disturbance, the dirt was crumbling, as if there were things squirming underneath. Far away, Harv had forgotten all about her.

Something stung her on the ankle. A snake must have bit her, but no way could a snake's fangs pierce her boot. The sound grew into a high-pitched scream as more things emerged from the soil around her.

Ramsey ran away, and four miles later she got to the Blazer covered in sweat and grime, with the first rays of dawn shining through the trees.

CHAPTER 8

MAXWELL CAME IN ten minutes before eight, unusually early.

He went into the break room and put his sack lunch in the mini fridge, then poured himself a cup of coffee and strolled up the hall to the dispatch room. He found Ramsey sitting behind the desk, hands folded on her lap, staring at the dusty computer screen on the desk. Maxwell sipped his coffee and looked at her. She didn't move.

"Are you okay?" he said.

Ramsey looked up at him. She said nothing.

"Have you been crying?"

She blinked. "What? No."

"It's just that your eyes are all red. You had a long night?"

"Uneventful. I'm bored."

"Well, get on. Get some sleep. Go get a pedicure or something. Relax."

She blinked again. "You got it."

Ramsey got up and walked out of the room, making stiff movements even though her muscles ached. She hadn't hiked that much in years, and her ankle felt like it was on fire. Out in the parking lot, she sat in the Blazer for a while in silence, taking stock of the night's events while trying not to hyperventilate. It all ended an hour ago when she pulled into the station's lot, hurried inside to clean up, change her clothes, plug the phone back in, and sit down right as Maxwell was walking in the door.

She told herself a hundred times how stupid she was. Her so-called mission amounted to a get-rich-quick scheme dreamed up while she was tweaking. But some reckless ambition wasn't the problem. Killing a meth cook, torturing him, and taking his money didn't weigh on her conscience one bit. What bothered her was that when the time came to execute the plan . . . she hesitated. In that moment when Harv turned to see her with his glowing white eyes, she choked.

And it was from there that it all went wrong.

She tried not to think about Harv and Willis being at each other's throats.

Tried not to think how she'd put herself right in the middle of it.

And she refused to think about the thing she found latched to her ankle, biting her, sucking her blood.

❋❋❋

Ramsey wasn't sure how she'd react when she got back to the safety of her trailer. The mask she wore in public was screwed on so tight there she usually wasn't sure what she felt until she was back in that sanctuary. This time she would probably freak out. She might get so scared that she'd kill herself after all.

She decided to get high, and didn't even take her uniform off to do it. She deserved to have some clothes ruined. She'd just tried to assassinate a man she barely knew for some money that she wasn't sure he had. And she was going to use *her own gun*. Any dipshit stickup man knew better. She sat on the sofa like a junkie, smoking bowl after bowl and feeling sorry for herself.

After an hour she forced herself off the couch, her muscles as thick as molasses. She threw away her uniform and took a few gulps of orange juice that made her stomach turn.

Finally, she returned to the duffel bag on the kitchen table.

Time to unpack.

She unzipped the bag, took out her black fatigues and her old boots, one of them sliced up around the ankle. She tossed them aside in disgust, then flung the night vision goggles down with them. Then she took out the black satchel. When she lifted it, the fabric undulated like some kind of alien seed pod. The thing from Harv's field was inside, the thing that had bit her ankle.

The movements grew quicker and the satchel swayed back and forth in Ramsey's hand. A pale white spike pierced through the black fabric and she hurried to the kitchen sink and held the satchel over it. More spikes poked through the fabric, squirming as they protruded and reached beyond the bag. The spikes bent and curled and flicked, ripping apart the satchel until the thing fell out into the sink and Ramsey was left holding a fistful of tattered black fabric.

She peered into the sink at the thing. It was as big as a softball, and heavy, covered in papery skin that was rich brown with dark freckles. The white spikes sprouted from random spots on its hide. The spikes were roots, with stubby branches splitting off from each one, wiggling in the air. Those stringy tentacles had torn the satchel's fabric, Ramsey's boot, and even her skin. She remembered the potato's bite, cutting into her flesh like razor wire. But it didn't cut her deeply. The roots wrapped themselves around her ankle and seemed to stop searching, content to cut into and draw blood.

Blood that never filled her boot, because the potato drank it.

Ramsey watched the bloodsucking potato in her sink for several minutes. The roots reached along the steel of the sink, some of them disappearing down the drain, but soon they stopped searching. The roots went still and eventually Ramsey took a wooden spoon and nudged it. Still no movement.

This was the evil shit Harv was doing, the secret he was keeping from the sheriff, the thing that scared Rubin Music enough to bring the law down on all their heads. And Harv's field was full of them. Thousands. Ramsey remembered him down in the dirt, trying to replant the squealing potatoes she'd disturbed. He would probably think that Willis had sent her to assassinate him. He'd blame the sheriff, and then Willis would be onto her in no time. She'd get caught.

But even that wasn't the real problem. The problem was that no one would believe this, just like she didn't believe Rubin Music.

Maybe she wouldn't have to explain herself. Maybe Harv wouldn't confront Willis. Maybe he'd rather keep it secret. Maybe he wouldn't even tell his new partner, the scary motherfucker.

Probably he would.

Ramsey was part of the mess now, and if she

wanted to survive she couldn't get caught standing still. A war was about to break out in Whaley County. She had to do something or else she'd be just another body littering the battlefield.

She went to the backdoor of the trailer, where she kept her gardening tools. She returned to the kitchen with a half-full bag of soil. She lifted the bag and poured the dirt into the sink, burying the potato. It was her only evidence, so she had to keep it alive.

She watched, and after a few minutes the mound of dirt twitched. The potato was alive in there, sucking up nutrients from the soil.

Ramsey was equally relieved and terrified. She puked up the orange juice and it splashed across the floor. She wiped her mouth and went for her bottle of painkillers. She dry-swallowed a handful and went to bed with the chemicals forcing her eyes shut.

***

Ramsey stumbled out of her bedroom in the afternoon. She entered the kitchen and ignored the circle of orange puke on the linoleum. She made herself a pot of coffee and only when she had the cup in her hand did she turn her attention to the potato.

The thing had doubled in size, sitting in the dirt now instead of beneath it, staring up at her with a pair of sprouts on the front of its head. More tentacles sprouted from its top, and larger ones on either side of its body, like arms. They flexed, and the little spikes rippled like underwater hair follicles. Ramsey downed the last of her coffee and went back into the bedroom. She returned with her shotgun, and pointed it down at the little brown creature in her sink. She stood there for an hour, waiting for the thing to jump at her so she could destroy it. It was evidence, but it could also kill her, and she'd made enough stupid mistakes already.

Instead of jumping the thing made a noise with a small orifice below its spiky eye stalks. The little mouth opened and closed, emanating an ugly squeak. It sputtered and whimpered, sounding too much like a baby. Ramsey hated babies.

She lowered the shotgun and whispered, "What the fuck are you?"

The potato whined and whimpered.

"What do you want?"

The whimpering got worse. Ramsey finally noticed that the soil she'd poured into the sink was dried out and dusty. The potato had sucked out all its moisture and nutrients.

"You want food. Ugh."

She opened the fridge and took out a pudding pack, peeled off the lid and tossed the open cup into the dirt next to the potato. One of its tentacles reached into the open cup and dipped into the pudding. Ramsey watched, amazed, as the pudding was vacuumed out of its plastic container within seconds. Every fibrous spike of the potato's roots seemed to suck up the food like a straw. The walls of the container were wiped clean and the potato let out a happy burp from its little mouth.

Ramsey puked up her coffee, covering the orange puke already on the floor. Her teeth slipped out and clattered through the puddle. "Fuck!" she yelled.

The spud goblin flinched at the sound. Ramsey picked up her teeth and hurried into the living room for her pipe. She smoked and tried to think. Even if the thing didn't hop out of the sink and try to kill her, what would she do with it? It was evidence that implicated Harv in a crime against . . . well, against nature. But who the hell would she show it to?

She paced back and forth in the living room, and didn't see the potato climb out of the sink and down to the floor. The spud goblin's tentacles slipped around on the kitchen linoleum, steering itself into the puddle of coffee and orange juice vomit. It rolled in the sticky mess and its tentacles slurped up the liquids within moments. It wiped the floor clean and grew bigger. It heard Ramsey's footsteps and crawled into the living room to find her.

Ramsey collapsed on the couch and placed her pipe on the coffee table as the potato approached from behind her. It maneuvered its way around the couch and

came to the coffee table, its roots reaching over the edge to feel out the tabletop. The tentacles jumbled over Ramsey's pipe and lighter until one of them rested on the plastic baggie full of her meth. The spiky root sliced through the plastic, reaching in to grip the chunks of crystal. Ramsey turned her head just in time to see it happen.

The potato's skin bubbled and twitched. Its spines stood straight and then quivered, and the orifice on its face let out a screech. Before Ramsey could say, "shit," her entire stash was gone, sucked up and ingested by the spud goblin.

The potato creature fell back against the floor, then rolled across the carpet and bumped into the far wall. Ramsey pulled herself to her feet as the creature batted its tentacles against the wall, following it into the corner across the room and then back again, hopping up and down like a hyperactive child, hammering out a savage tribal beat against the drywall. Ramsey dove for the potato, trying to catch it, and succeeded in denting the drywall with her head.

The potato emitted a warbling roar, then slammed its basketball-sized body into the opposite wall, somehow hard enough for Ramsey's TV to fall off its mounting and crash against the floor.

Ramsey staggered to her feet. She gave up on catching the creature. Instead, she ran into her bedroom to hide. The potato followed her, ramming the door open with its body. It knocked over a dresser and climbed onto the bed, its tentacles ripping the bedspread Ramsey had slept under as a girl. Ramsey's breathing quickened in panic and she clutched at her hair with both hands. She watched the thing rampage through the room and knew then that she'd finally gone crazy. Even trying to remember where she'd put the shotgun brought no results to her mind. Her brain refused to think. She could only let her bear witness to the little abomination wrecking her bedroom.

The spud goblin flopped back and forth on the bed and finally came right at her. She let out a yelp as it dove between her legs and back into the living room again. The creature flopped into the kitchen and crashed through a cupboard door, setting the pots and pans banging around, then crashed onto the linoleum again.

Ramsey peeked into the kitchen to see the destruction, but perked up when she saw the duffel bag on the table. The Glock. Hopefully she wasn't too impaired to hit such a small and fast target.

She dashed across the room for the bag, jumping high over the little cartwheeling monstrosity. She reached the bag and opened it, saw the Glock sitting alone at the bottom. She took it in hand, flicked off the safety, and turned back to the spud goblin, lying on the floor and spinning itself around with its leg tentacles, like a disgusting little Curly from *The Three Stooges*. Ramsey lined the potato up in her sights and it stopped spinning. It sat up to face her, its eye sprouts pointing at the gun. The moment was so quiet that Ramsey could hear herself breathing.

She was still hyperventilating.

Ramsey lowered the gun and screamed at the spud goblin, full throated, a primal roar that caused the little creature to cringe away from her. She flicked the safety back on and slammed the Glock on the kitchen table, then took the empty duffel bag and held it open. She came toward the potato and the creature scurried up to meet her. It hopped into the darkness of the bag and Ramsey zipped it shut.

The spud goblin tussled and squealed for a few moments, then settled down and purred in comfort.

CHAPTER 9

THE HOUSE WAS a mess and the potato kept moaning for food. Ramsey threw pudding packs into the duffel bag every few minutes to keep it quiet while she tried to clean up.

She took out her cell phone and dialed the station. LaGrange picked up and she told him she had the flu. He believed the lie, and even bitched at her for making him cover her shift.

Ramsey put on some fresh clothes and pinned up her hair. She put her Glock in a shoulder holster beneath her jacket and took the duffel bag with her. The potato couldn't leave her sight until she figured out what to do with it, but first came a greater priority.

She had to re-up her stash.

She usually visited Bugs at night, but this was an emergency. Bugs was a Mexican kid she'd known since high school. Ramsey and Bugs reconnected when she'd gotten the taste for meth. Someone hooked her up with him and his supply line was just the way Ramsey liked it: regular. Ramsey called him up for an ounce at the end of every month and Bugs never let her down. She trusted him to provide her medicine, and he was the only one who knew about it. She depended on him so much he might as well be her life partner.

These days Bugs had a legit job at a call center for some insurance corporation that only knew him as Antonio. He lived in a dilapidated apartment block on a highway lined with brightly colored truck stops and taverns. She called him on the way over, and soon she was zooming into the lot and screeching into a parking space as inconspicuously as she could. Ramsey cut the Blazer's engine and walked across the parking lot to Bugs' door.

Bugs opened his door for her and gave her a one-armed hug just for appearances, taking care to avoid her shoulder holster. He loomed over her, standing six-and-a-half feet tall with floppy white sneakers on his gigantic feet. Bugs had caramel-colored skin and a shaggy black Mohawk on top of his head that he combed down at his day job. Ramsey always thought he looked like his namesake, a lanky cartoon rabbit who could never get caught. She let him hug her for a moment before stepping away as he locked the door.

"How you doin'?" he asked, taking a seat on his sofa and digging out his gear from the coffee table.

Ramsey crouched down and leaned back against the wall next to the door. "Long story. I'm real sorry about this. I usually like to keep things steady."

"It's cool. You okay?"

"Yeah, I'm . . . I'm losing it a little bit."

He held up the baggy and started tying it shut. "You smokin' too much of this?"

"Every little bit of that stuff is too much."

He tossed the bag across the room. Ramsey caught it and stuffed it into the pocket of her cargo pants.

He looked at her with his droopy eyes. "You wanna talk about it?"

"What? No."

"I'm just sayin' be careful."

"I am. I'm just . . . under a lot of stress."

Bugs nodded, still looking at her. He let the room be silent until Ramsey felt like elaborating. "I never stick my nose into things," she said. There was weariness in her voice. "You know who I work for. I don't make waves for him. All sorts of nefarious shit's come and gone over the years, and I stayed the fuck out of it every time. But now . . . I wasn't thinking straight." Ramsey stopped herself. She was talking about her problems to her drug dealer. She really was losing it.

She stood up, reached into her jacket, and took out a stack of twenties folded in half. She stepped over to Bugs and handed him the money. "Here you go, man. I can't tell you how much I appreciate this."

Bugs smiled up at her. "You always say that."

As he took the money, a roar came from outside the apartment. Bugs looked through the window blinds and saw a giant truck hop the sidewalk in front of his apartment and lurch to a stop. "Oh, fuck," he said as the doors opened and three men piled out. Bugs went for his pistol in the coffee table but they were already kicking in the door.

Just as Ramsey was reaching for her Glock, one of the intruders was on her. He tackled her to the ground but she already had her arms hooked beneath his. She rolled him over her and came to a rest straddling his chest. It was the greasy guy from the White Star Range, staring at the crotch of her pants with a shit-eating grin.

She punched him in the face but heard a quick sucking sound half a second long. Ramsey looked up to see Bugs lying face down on his sofa, bleeding out the back of his head. Standing over him, holding a silenced pistol, was the dad from the gun range. Ramsey's bloodshot eyes widened at him.

The redhead boy approached her, pointing his own pistol. He pointed to his friend on the floor. "Get off him," he said.

"Or get me off," said the greasy guy, chuckling.

Ramsey raised her hands and stood up, keeping her eyes on Bugs' murderer. She ignored the other two, and she ignored Bugs' body, because she knew if she saw it she'd remember young Antonio from high school, how tall and smart he'd been. What a good friend he'd been to her. She glared at his shooter, the wrinkles around his eyes that looked like slashes in his skin, the jean shorts and Nikes and another goddamn pastel polo shirt. She imagined him wearing his Easter best while she strangled the life out of him.

The man looked back at her and flicked his gun at the body on the couch. "You mad that I killed this spic?"

"Very," said Ramsey.

"Figures. Let's go."

The greasy guy took hold of Ramsey's wrists and brought them behind her back to restrain her with a zip tie. He did the same to her ankles. The redhead moved over and reached into Ramsey's jacket, careful not to touch her body as he did so. His hand took the Glock out of her shoulder holster and put it in the back of his belt. He reached into her pants pocket, visibly uncomfortable, and took out her car keys. She watched as he tossed the keys to his partner. The two of them then took her by the elbows and lifted, carrying her out of Bugs' apartment.

They dragged her to the chromed-out truck. The older man climbed into the driver's seat as Ramsey was carried around back. Around the apartment block, residents stood in their doorways or out on their balconies, summoned by the loud bluster of the truck's V8. They watched the two boys carry Ramsey by her shoulders and legs. Ramsey scanned the crowd. None of them looked interested in helping her.

The two boys opened the steel toolbox mounted in the truck bed. It was empty. "Don't put me in that box," Ramsey said.

"You have to go in the box," the redhead answered softly. Ramsey didn't argue with him. She let the boys lay her in the metal coffin and closed her eyes as the lid clanked shut on top of her.

CHAPTER 10

RAMSEY COULDN'T TELL where they were going, no matter how much she tried to track the turns. She could only wait until the truck stopped and the engine shut off. They were in a room with an echo. She heard the buzz and rattle of an electric garage door closing. When the door shut, she heard people climbing into the truck bed. The lock turned and the top of the toolbox creaked open.

Ramsey squinted against the fluorescent lighting above. Within the light she saw the redhead's square face. He reached down and gently hooked his hands in her armpits. Ramsey went limp and let him pull her up out of the toolbox. The teenager was deceptively strong, but still looked like he was sorry for touching her. He sat Ramsey down in the truck bed and she blinked her eyes clear and took a quick glance at her surroundings.

They were in a big six-car garage, empty except for the truck and Ramsey's Blazer. The walls were painted bright white, and mounted all around were fishing poles, deer heads, a set of compound bows, two kayaks, a pegboard with a set of expensive power tools dangling from it, and over by the door to enter the house, a rebel flag.

Ramsey turned her attention to her captors. The older man stood at the tailgate while the teenagers sat on sides of the truck bed, leaning forward on their knees and staring down at her. Ramsey promised herself that a chance would come to strike back. She just had to be ready for it. She had a four-inch knife in her right boot. She doubted that she could kill all three of them with her hands tied behind her back, but if she could just reach the knife and cut the zip tie, she'd at least have a chance.

She focused her mind and nodded to the older man at the tailgate. "Who the fuck are you people?" she said to him.

"My name's John," he said. He pointed to the redhead and then the greasy guy. "That's my son Justin, and that's Frank. We want to ask you a few questions."

"You killed my friend and kidnapped me. You brought me back to your home and you just told me your names, which means you're not letting me leave this garage alive."

"She's a hardass, alright," said Frank, combing his hair behind his ears.

"Quiet," John told him. "We want to talk to you about our friend Ruby. He went into the sheriff's station and never came out. Word is you're the one he talked to. What happened to him in there?"

"I don't know," she said.

"I don't believe that. Just like I don't believe the sheriff's account of it. I think Willis tortured that poor boy. I think he killed him and he's tryin' to put the blame on you."

"Then take all this up with him."

"I would have. But you're the one who came snooping around the range. Why?"

"I wanted to know who it was I killed."

"So you did kill him!" Frank said. He must have been close to Music.

"I did," she admitted, "but it was an accident."

"How's that work?" John said.

Ramsey turned back to the old man. "He attacked me, so I retaliated. He died from a concussion."

"Police fuckin' brutality."

"Crazy fucking tweaker," Ramsey replied. "He was scared shitless and paranoid as hell. He attacked me."

Frank was about to retort before John held up a hand to silence him. "What was he paranoid about? What did he say to you?"

"Nothing."

"She's lying," Justin said in a gentle voice. Ramsey eyed him.

"Let's say you're telling the truth," John said. "You ain't outta the woods yet. Because even if all that was an accident, why did you try to kill Harv? Before you answer, just know that we've been following you. We know you left the station last night for a few hours. Then we have Harv calling us, bitching about how he nearly got shot by . . . what was it?"

"He said it was a ninja," Justin said.

Ramsey glared into John's pale brown eyes, gritting her teeth. "It was a stupid idea," she said. "Thought I could rob him but it turned out he ain't got shit out there. I changed my mind and took off."

John seemed to consider her words, but she knew he didn't believe her.

"Think this through," she said. "I'm just a deputy. I got no say in this county. Willis Ruth is running the show and he don't trust me. He keeps me around because I kick ass and I'm a war hero. I make his operation look good. He don't know nothing, and as far as he knows, I don't know nothing either. And if Willis finds out I tried to steal from his operation, I'm done for anyway."

"So we should just let you go, huh?" John said.

"I'm just sayin' that if you kill me like Harv wants you to, it'll start a war between him and the sheriff, and the sheriff'll win. Then where will you guys be?"

Justin cleared his throat. "You think we work for Harv?"

Ramsey looked back at him. "Don't you?"

"Harv works for us," said John.

"But he owns the land," said Ramsey. "He owns the gun range, doesn't he?"

"It's in his name, sure. But he ain't running the show here. Things are different now. The way Harv and Willis run things has worked well enough, but the two of them are happy just to sell crank and make money. They brought us on board a few years ago, and while I respect their business acumen, both of 'em are nothing more than country-fried crooks. They got no vision. But we do. We're the ones that got Harv to help us with a special project . . . and I suspect you know what that project is. You ran through Harv's field. You saw it, didn't you?"

"Look . . . " she started, but another voice echoed off the garage walls, cutting her off.

"No more lies."

Everyone looked across the garage as a man entered from the door next to the rebel flag. He stepped around the truck and stood next to John. He gripped the tailgate with one hand and swung his body up with one arm like a gymnast to sit on the fender. The man was short and bulky, with dense muscles knotted beneath his skin. He wore black tactical pants and a tattered denim vest covered in what looked like merit badges with weird runes on them. A strip on the chest said his name was Werewolf, though his head was so bald it shined. He had sharp cheekbones and eyes that were wide open and clear, staring at her like a hawk. He had the bulk of a prisoner and the eyes of a psychotic, and completing the look were the tattoos spilling out across his skin. They covered his neck and arms with wild portraits like dragon-wrapped swastikas, barbed wire fists, Jesus wrapped in the Gadsden flag, and Donald Trump with a halo. Little bullets cascaded between all the portraits.

Werewolf locked his eyes on Ramsey. She met his gaze and forced herself not to blink. This was the guy who scared Rubin Music into turning snitch. Ramsey took a deep, silent breath and tugged against her zip ties.

Werewolf watched her quietly struggle and scoffed to himself. "People think things are getting better," he said. "But everything is shit. It's the worst shit of all time. And nobody sees it. They're content with a slow slide into filth. Our world is a rotting carcass, and as it rots, it *expands*. It fills up with noxious shit. Loses its purity. Some people call it progress, but it's actually the bloat of a corpse. And everybody's fooled themselves into thinking it's a good thing."

He stopped, as if waiting for her to answer. Ramsey shrugged at him.

"Exactly," said Werewolf. "The system depends on what you just did there. They need us to shrug and sit back and let the rot do its work. Everybody just relaxes and buys into it. We're becoming more tolerant, more sentimental. We corrupt ourselves with foreign elements and everyone things its just change. But it's not. It's a mutation. It's the symptoms of disease. Truth is we've thrown away our purity in exchange for blasphemy and rot. And nobody wants to think about what it'd take to make this country *alive again*. They tranquilize themselves with childish media and processed food and—"

"You're full of shit," Ramsey stated. "That tranquilized enough for you?" She looked around at the other three men. John, Justin, and Frank were all looking down at her, solemnly listening to the biker's speech. "Just because you convinced these fellas of something doesn't mean shit to me."

"How would you know anything?" Werewolf said. "You're a part of the system. You were a Marine, right? Bet you were good at it. An obedient little dog. What do they do in the military? Break you down so they can build you up again the way they see fit. From what I understand, you're the only real law in this county. The sheriff don't count. All your actions against us are just the system trying to defend itself."

"That's why you're going to kill me."

"Yep."

"Let me say something first?"

Werewolf held out a hand for her to proceed.

"You say that Harv works for you guys instead of the other way around, but I don't think your bike club knows what you're doing out here, Mr. Werewolf. It looks like you're trying to take over Whaley County's meth trade and cut out Sheriff Ruth. But Rubin Music got spooked and tried to warn him. So the truth is you're lucky that I wound up killing him."

"Fuck you!" Frank spat.

Werewolf leaned toward Ramsey. "I don't give a shit who's the candy man out here in the sticks, so your theory ain't shit. And you know that, don't you? You know I'm not trying to horn in on the drug trade. You've seen it, haven't you?"

Ramsey's left eye twitched and her lip quivered. She closed her eyes and tried to relax as she hooked a fingertip into her right boot, inching it closer to the knife. "I don't know what I saw," she muttered. "But I got . . . pictures of it."

"Where?"

"In my car. A bag in the backseat."

Werewolf gave a nod and Justin slipped off the truck and walked over to the Blazer. He reached into the backseat and brought out the duffel bag. "It's heavy," he said. Justin shook the bag and it wiggled in his grip. He held it up for the others to see and they leaned back as if astonished.

"Ain't no pictures in there, girl," said Frank.

"She took one of 'em," said John.

Werewolf smiled with sharp, narrow teeth. "You stupid bitch. You're about to see some shit firsthand now. Bring that up here."

Justin climbed back onto the truck and gave the wiggling duffel bag to Werewolf. The biker stood up in the bed of the truck and held the bag over Ramsey's head. He began to pull on the zipper and the bag stopped wiggling. A white tentacle snaked out of the small opening and waved back and forth. A growl like an angry cat being forced into the bathtub emanated from the bag. Werewolf held the bag out over Ramsey's head. "Remember what I said about the system? This is where it gets you, bitch."

Werewolf pulled the zipper and the potato

creature plopped out of the duffel bag. It fell onto Ramsey's head and its web of white tentacles gripped her dark hair. Ramsey squeezed her eyes shut as the creature hugged her head and she felt its hot french fry breath coating her face.

She expected the spud goblin to do to her what it had done to the pudding packs. But the creature only clutched at Ramsey's hair and then climbed down her body, hanging from her neck and shoulders with its spiky appendages. The four men edged away to the tailgate of the truck, watching the spud goblin, waiting for it to strike, but instead it curled itself up in Ramsey's lap and wiggled comfortably. Its breathy hiss softened to an alien purr.

"It's just sitting there!" Frank said. "The fuck's wrong with it?"

John patted Werewolf on the arm. "Is that how it's supposed to be?" he whispered.

Werewolf glared at the squirming thing in Ramsey's lap, then raised his eyes to look at her. She stared back, perfectly still. "Well, boys," he said, "this one's defective."

"What did you do to it, girl?" said Werewolf.

"You think I know what the fuck is going on here?"

"Alright," he said. "Let's get this over with." Werewolf reached beneath his vest, pulled out a nickel-plated forty-five, and handed it to Frank. Frank stood up on the truck bed and pointed the gun down at Ramsey's head, a crooked sneer spreading across his face.

The spud goblin turned in Ramsey's lap and growled up at Frank. Its tentacle spikes went stiff. It shifted its weight around on its roots, then pounced from Ramsey's lap and wrapped itself around Frank's arm.

Frank screamed and spun around, trying to shake the thing off and accidentally clotheslining Justin off the truck. Frank's angry roar turned into a high pitched shriek as the potato's roots sliced into his arm like cutting a cake. Every spike and spine sheared him with the easiest touch, shaving off hunks of skin as it climbed up the arm. By the time the spud goblin got to Frank's shoulder, his appendage had been reduced to ribbons of red meat and perfectly sliced bone. The bloody mess dangled down to Frank's knees and his shrieking faded to silence right as he lost consciousness from shock and fell over the edge of the truck bed to the concrete below. The spud goblin fell with him, clawing at Frank's face with its razor sharp roots.

Ramsey stared at the puddle of minced flesh in front of her. The nickel-plated forty-five lay in the mess of meat and blood. She couldn't see over the edge of the truck, but could hear the spud goblin moving around. It chuckled and slobbered and splashed around in something wet. Only a few seconds had passed, because by then the guns were out.

Ramsey flattened herself against the truck bed as John began shooting. She saw his head just over the tailgate, with shells popping up in front of him. The gunshots filled the garage with noise, mixed with the potato's savage snarl. Suddenly John's head fell from Ramsey's sight. Then he screamed, and a jet of crimson splashed up onto the garage door. Ramsey lay in the truck bed and watched the blood drip down the door's interior. She heard the wet slopping sound of flesh melting away, the low buzz of bones being pulped and absorbed at the potato's touch.

CHAPTER 11

SOON THE SPUD goblin climbed back into the truck bed, now the size of a Labrador, and curled up against her. It purred into her stomach, snuggling against her, yawning with its giant spike-filled mouth.

Ramsey tried not to disturb the creature as she slid the knife out of her boot with her fingertips. She cut the zip ties and freed herself, then pushed the spud goblin out of her lap. She poked her head up to look around the garage. The room was quiet. Werewolf was nowhere to be seen. The door next to the rebel flag was still open. He must have escaped.

Ramsey clutched the knife in her hand and moved to the tailgate. She looked over the edge at the bodies on the floor. The spud goblin had soaked up most of the blood, leaving just a few smears on the concrete. Justin lay dead on the ground with a gaping hole in his torso, like the goblin had burrowed through his ribcage and sucked out his organs. Frank was next to him, missing his head and arm. John lay near the garage door, the front half of his body peeled open like a sardine can. All of their wounds were made of thousands of fillet cuts that swirled and flowed and created the image of blossoming flesh. The spud goblin had mutilated them beautifully.

Ramsey hopped out of the truck and went to Justin's body to retrieve her gun. She crept over to the open door that led into the house and peeked around the edge. Still no sign of Werewolf. John's place was one of those houses that was trying to be in a beauty pageant. There were columns and balconies and multiple stairways that curled around to all the different floors, and on every wall there were giant family photos full of redheads.

Ramsey went outside and saw a panel of buttons next to the door. She pressing them with the barrel of her gun and all six of the garage doors clanked their way open.

She went back to the truck bed and found the spud goblin still inside, napping. It was more oval shaped now, with its wide mouth of fangs positioned near the top of its body. Its array of spiky tentacles had woven themselves together to form four long limbs, with dozens more eyes sprouting from the rest of its body, mostly gathered at the top of its head like hair.

Ramsey retrieved her sheriff's department jacket from her Blazer and bundled the creature up in it. She lifted it into her arms and dumped the beast into her backseat, then climbed behind the wheel. She backed out of the garage and drove down a long concrete driveway. John's home was in some fancy subdivision that Ramsey didn't recognize. It was a maze of streets with whimsical names, and after too many turns, she finally found the highway and realized that she was in Tyrell County, about an hour from home. She kept her eyes and ears open, scanning every road for a motorcycle. Werewolf could be anywhere, and at any moment he could ride up next to the Blazer and put a bullet in her head. It was a long drive to her house.

When she arrived, she bypassed her street and drove to a rutted dirt trail half a mile down the highway. That road led her to a cow field where she parked under a thicket of trees.

Ramsey took the baggie Bugs had given her out of her cargo pocket. She untied the knot and sprinkled a pile of crystal onto her driver's license. She pressed the card against her thigh and crushed the crystal with the flat of her knife. She formed a line and lifted the card up to her face, snorted loudly. The spud grumbled sleepily in the back seat. Ramsey looked back to see it drooling white slime on her jacket.

"You saved my ass," she whispered to it. "So thanks. I think . . . I'm gonna call you Spudley. Okay."

Ramsey wiped her nose and sniffled, then climbed out of the Blazer as quietly as she could. She hiked across the cow field and into the trees on the other side. A quarter mile through was her property line. She approached slowly, peering through the trees until she could see her trailer's roof. She moved through the brush to get a better view and saw Werewolf's motorcycle in her driveway.

At least now she knew where he was.

She waited, watched. After a few minutes, the biker kicked the front door outward and stomped down Ramsey's porch steps. He mounted his bike and roared away up the street.

There was no time to waste. Ramsey ran out of the woods and through the yard. Luckily, the door was already open. Inside was what she expected. Werewolf had turned the house upside down. The few pieces of furniture Ramsey had were overturned. Holes had been punched through the black-painted walls. Every nook and cranny had been excavated, with papers and junk spread across the floors. Ramsey figured that the damage from Spudley's rampage was negated now.

Ramsey stepped through the mess and headed for the bedroom. It had been destroyed. Her closet was open and her uniforms had been ripped off their hangers and sliced up with a knife. He'd even cut up her mattress. Her bedside cabinet had been opened and all the paraphernalia had been spilled out. Werewolf might not have given a damn about her gear, but Ramsey did. She gathered it all up into a plastic bag as a plan began to form in her mind.

She realized that Werewolf might still be out there, watching the house, waiting for her to return. She didn't hear a motorcycle but she hurried just the same. She checked her hiding spots, but Werewolf had found her dad's old shotgun, her ammo, and her spare Glock. It was all gone. The only weapon she had was the taser hidden on top of the cupboard, fully charged. Ramsey marched into the kitchen and picked up the house phone.

She dialed the sheriff's station.

LaGrange answered.

Ramsey held the phone out and smashed a few coffee cups on the floor. Then she pulled out her Glock and fired two rounds through the roof.

She dropped the phone and ran.

CHAPTER 12

BY THE TIME she got back to the Blazer she had seven messages on her cell phone. The first two were from LaGrange and the rest were from Sheriff Ruth himself. Her lack of response would only alarm them more. They were on their way to her place.

Good.

She drove back through the logging trail with Spudley still sleeping in the backseat. She threw the plastic bag full of her gear into a ditch, but she kept the pipe. She smoked as she drove across the county, even though it was broad daylight, and reassessed her plan. The first thing to do was find Doug Crosby. He was the only one she could trust now. She sat in the parking lot of an abandoned hardware store and smoked, listening to Spudley snore in the darkness of her jacket.

When the sun began to set, she looked up Crosby's address on her phone and tapped it into the GPS. He lived on a quiet suburban street on the north side of Whaley County. Ramsey approached the Crosby house and knocked on the door. It opened to the noise of five children under one roof. Standing in the doorway was Doug's wife, Heather. Heather remembered Ramsey from high school and she gave her a subtle scowl of contempt. Ramsey barely noticed. She spoke so fast, Heather didn't get a chance to interrupt.

"Hello, ma'am. My name's Violet Ramsey, I'm a deputy with the sheriff's department. Is Douglas home? I actually need to speak with him. I'm really sorry, I know it's late, but it's about an official investigation and we're in need of his expertise. I really hope it won't take much time."

The speech was quick and punchy. She'd practiced it many times and it still made her feel like a homeless lady begging for change. She wondered if Heather could tell how high she was. "Just a moment," she said, and shut the door in Ramsey's face.

It was a long minute before Doug stepped out onto the porch. "Violet? What's going on?" he said. Doug was twice her size, looking down at her with deep concern through his thick horn-rimmed glasses. He wore sweatpants and a t-shirt like he was at a slumber party. Doug crossed his big arms and shifted his weight, sizing Ramsey up, probably guessing that she was high.

"Well, I'll be honest, Doug," Ramsey said with a sniffle. "This isn't official but it is critical. You're the only one in Whaley County I can trust since my drug dealer got killed."

"Your what?"

"If I could, I'd be hiring him for this mission, believe me. But they blew his brains out right in fuckin' front of me."

"You mean Antonio? I saw that on—"

"Don't worry about it," she said. "There's no time. And it ain't the weirdest thing I'm going to tell you. You know Harv Hallihan? He's setting up a terrorist attack. I need your guns to stop him."

"My guns?"

"Yeah, how many guns do you have?"

Crosby uncrossed his arms and put them in his pockets. "What kind of terrorist plot is gonna happen in Whaley County?"

"Yeah, that's a good point. But I can show you proof and then you'll believe me. Come over to my car."

She got halfway down the steps before he said, "I'm not leaving this porch."

Ramsey turned and took a deep breath. She tried to slow herself down, remind herself to help Doug catch up. "Doug," she said, "I know how this all looks. But you . . . you probably know me better than anybody in this community. That ain't saying much, but . . . I'm begging you, man. Just please look in the backseat of my car."

Doug rocked back and forth on his bare feet. "Alright, Ramsey," he said. "I'll take a look. But unless it blows my mind, then I have to go back inside."

They walked out across the lawn to Ramsey's Blazer. Crosby slowed as he saw the toddler-sized figure sitting in the back. It wore a sheriff's jacket, but its arms were long white tentacles covered in spikes, and its head was a misshapen lump that twisted around to look through the window at him. Crosby stopped in his tracks. Two fat tentacles pressed against the glass and the creature's mouth gaped open, baring jagged fangs and panting like a dog.

"Your mind blown?" Ramsey said.

Crosby backed away from the Blazer and took a few breaths. "What's going on here?" he said as calmly as he could. "Lay it all out."

"This thing's some kind of biological weapon.

Harv Hallihan made it for this biker guy named Werewolf. Serious anti-government shit. When this thing gets going, it cuts through people like a hot knife. When it touches anything, like, organic . . . it absorbs it like a sponge. That's how it eats. What would happen if a few hundred of these things were running around free?"

"Well, why isn't this one?"

"I don't know, it's . . . it's been kinda docile so far . . . but it's been out for a day and look at the size of it! And it could turn on me at some point, easily."

"Why aren't you going to your boss, then?" said Crosby. "Sheriff Ruth?"

"Yeah."

"Because he and Harv are partners! But I don't think he's onto Harv yet. If he was . . . to the sheriff this is all business, and weapons of mass destruction are bad for business. He can't have the damn Department of Homeland Security comin' to Whaley County. No, when he gets wind of all this, he's gonna kill everybody to cover his tracks. And if he realizes that I'm involved? He'll kill me too. Just business."

"He'd really kill you? He's as bad as they say he is?"

Ramsey nodded.

"So what's the plan?"

"I need some guns. I'm down to half a clip and a taser. I just need to take out Harv . . . and Werewolf . . . and get rid of these potato things . . . before the sheriff realizes what's up . . . so then I don't have to kill *him*. Then everything can go back to normal. And I'll have your guns back to you by morning."

"Okay," Crosby said. "Forget the fact that you're planning a killing spree, there's no way you're taking my guns."

"I'm just borrowing them!"

"You're high. I can tell."

"Fine. Come with me, then. You became an accessory as soon as you saw Spudley anyway."

"Spudley? You named it?"

"Yeah, he's ripped everything to shreds except me. We've bonded."

Crosby looked away for a few moments. Inside his pockets, his hands clenched and unclenched. "I've been a desk jockey too long. That must be why I'm considering this." He looked up at his home, the windows glowing and his family inside. "I need some excitement. But I gotta get back by six-thirty. Gotta get the kids ready for school. Nonnegotiable."

"Done. What're you packing?"

"I'll show you soon. I need five minutes to get myself together and explain to the wife."

"Tell her I'm your client."

"I can lie to my own wife, thank you." Crosby started walking away. Ramsey called after him.

"You got a truck or something we can take? They know my car."

"Yeah," he said, marching up to the house.

He came out five minutes later in sneakers and black jeans, wearing a dark blue Braves hoodie with is gun belt hidden beneath. He'd put in contact lenses and had a baseball cap pulled down low over his eyes. He went around the house and drove an old Chevy pickup out of the garage and followed Ramsey up the road. She left her Blazer parked behind a dimly lit Waffle House and loaded the spud goblin into Crosby's truck, sitting it in the middle seat between them.

"Where to?" Crosby said.

"My place."

CHAPTER 13

"**THIS TRUCK IS OLD,**" she said, drumming her fingers on her knee. "You must spend a lot tuning it up. This is a nice truck."

"I'm a small-town lawyer, but I'm still a lawyer. Are you just gonna smoke that right in front of me?"

Ramsey nodded, the glass pipe clenched in her gums. She lit up and drew in deeply, blew a cloud of pale smoke out the window. "Show me your guns."

He pulled them out for her. She reached around Spudley and took two Glocks from him, similar to her own. "No shotgun? We're storming a compound here."

"I've got my Desert Eagle and you can have those two. They're not registered so we can destroy them afterward. Plus, if we do this right we'll only fire two shots total."

Ramsey took another long drag on the pipe.

"Look," he said. "I'm not accusing you of anything but I checked the news before we left. Just today there was a triple murder in Tyrell County. And with Antonio killed on the same day, well . . . "

She blew out the smoke. "Thank you for not accusing me."

"Fair enough. But you know . . . you should

probably be paying me for this. For renting the guns. And for my mercenary services."

Ramsey cut her eyes at him and saw his face in the glow of his smartphone. His thumb danced across its bright surface while his eyes never left the road. He was cold and calm, exactly how she needed him.

"Sure," she said. "Harv's got money. We take him out and it's yours."

"Fifty-fifty?"

"Fuck it, you can have the whole pot. All I need is to keep my job. You can even stay out of the bloodshed if you like."

"Oh, I plan to." Crosby drove down Ramsey's street, where at the end they saw her trailer with two vehicles in the driveway, headlights on. "We've arrived," he said, putting away his phone.

"Just float us past 'em," Ramsey said, hunkering down in her seat and peeking out the window at her family's trailer. The porch light was on and all the windows were lit. Parked on the gravel driveway was a Charger painted Dukes of Hazzard orange and a squad car with its blue LED bar illuminating the trees. LaGrange leaned against the squad car smoking a cigarette, so Maxwell and Sheriff Ruth must be inside the trailer checking out the scene.

They drove by and a few miles down the street he pulled a k-turn and drove back. He cut the lights and rolled to a stop a hundred yards from Ramsey's driveway, around a curve where they could just barely see the blue lights through the trees. The spud goblin snarled in the darkness of the cab, bouncing in its seat and slapping its spiky root hands against its spiky root legs.

Crosby and Ramsey watched the headlights

through the trees. "What's going on in there?" he asked.

"They think I'm missing. I'm hoping this will keep them distracted long enough so everything can go smooth."

"Then why are we here?"

"I need to know who I'm dealing with. I think they know what Werewolf's deal is."

"So we're going to . . . "

"He's moving, let's go."

A pair of headlights ambled around Ramsey's yard and then up her driveway. The squad car turned onto the street and headed up the road.

Doug followed it across Whaley County to the sheriff's station. He parked across the street and they watched the squad car pull into the station's lot. Before Crosby could put the truck in park, the passenger door creaked open and Ramsey was gone. Crosby saw her out on the pavement, jogging toward the sheriff's station. He looked at the spud goblin sitting next to him. Its tentacle eyes turned toward him and waved like serpents. Its mouth stretched wide into a toothy smile that leaked white drool.

Crosby rested his hand on his Desert Eagle. He stole a glance across the street and saw Ramsey stab the deputy in the guts with her taser. There was a bright spark and the man doubled over in pain. Crosby put the truck in gear and drove over to intercept Ramsey. When he pulled up, she opened the door and shoved Duane Maxwell into the cab.

"Drive," she said.

✵✵✵

They took him to one of the strip malls situated on a piece of highway all by itself. Ramsey sat Maxwell down on the steps leading up to the back of the Dollar Store and cuffed him to the steel railing. Crosby stood by his truck just a few yards away. A spotlight mounted to his side mirror shined on Maxwell.

"What the fuck, Ramsey?" the deputy said in a weak voice.

"What the fuck indeed," Crosby added. Ramsey glanced back at him, her eyes wide with anger. He crossed his arms and leaned back against the truck.

She turned to Maxwell. "Listen," she said, "I need to know about Harv and those bikers. I know you know about it."

Maxwell looked up at her, blinking his eyes, his jaw slack. "What happened to you? We was . . . "

"I set you up. Answer my question."

"You vindictive bitch . . . . You . . . I mean, why you wanna know about the bikers? You always stayed outta the sheriff's business."

"Things are changing," she said. She nodded her head and Maxwell looked through the steel bars of the railing.

Spudley toddled around on the concrete next to the steps, testing out its feet. The fibrous white limbs had grown bigger and stronger. The potato's fanged mouth babbled sloppy words, like it had a baby's intelligence. Its long eyestalks gazed up at the stars and swayed in the night air.

"Holy shit . . . " Maxwell said.

"You know what it is, don't you?"

"No, I . . . " He looked up at her. "We knew he was . . . is *that* what Harv's making?"

"Tell me about the bikers," she said again.

"They, uh . . . called the White Dragons. Bunch of neo-nazi psychos. They run drugs from here to Texas. They buy Harv's shit and move it. Uncle Willis, he . . . "

"He runs security. Along with you and LaGrange."

Maxwell looked up at her and grimaced. "That's pretty much the business model, yeah."

"Only it's not going so smooth lately?"

"Naw . . . "

"Come on, Maxwell. I know you know. I need to know too." Ramsey lifted her hand and held Maxwell's own revolver an inch from his forehead.

Maxwell looked at her for several moments, then licked his lips. "We haven't heard from them the last few weeks. Then Uncle Willis found a news report from Montgomery. Nine members of the White Dragons got killed in a sports bar shootout. They were the captains. Rest of the gang's scattered to the winds now. The rumor is that one of the leaders took out all the others."

"Werewolf," she said.

"What the fuck is going on here, Ramsey? We thought you were killed in your home, now you're pointing my gun at me? We've always got along, haven't we? You never wanted to be involved in our shit and we always respected that, didn't we?"

"That's true."

"Then let me go!"

"I can't. This isn't personal, Duane. I first got caught up in all this because of Rubin Music. Now it's because of that thing over there. And I'm not out to take you guys down. I mean that, even if you don't believe it." She crouched down in front of him and gazed into his eyes. "But either way, the truth is that I'm a drug addict and I just can't afford to lose my job."

"What the fuck are you talking about? You sound crazy!"

Ramsey cocked her head at him. Maxwell had that desperate look in his eyes that she hated so much. He had it because all sense of control had been taken away from him. He was completely at her mercy. Her brain tingled with electricity. She was spinning hard, but unlike her colleague, she was still in control. There were crooked lawmen and skinheads and potato monsters all around her, but she was still in the driver's seat, goddammit. She could control this whole situation and return her life back to normal. She just had to be willing to do what was necessary.

Ramsey stood up and shot Maxwell in the head.

Crosby jumped at the gunshot. "The fuck are you doing?" he shouted, staring at the body slumping down on the concrete stairs. Maxwell's arms dangling by handcuffs from the steel railing, and blood ran down the steps below his head wound. Ramsey tossed the gun down at his feet and turned back to face Crosby. "He was a witness," she said. "And this'll slow down the sheriff even more."

Behind her, Spudley made a growling cry and shuffled over to the body. It reached its tentacle arm into the hole in Maxwell's head, first caressing the opening, then slipping inside, filling up his skull, absorbing everything it touched. The arm pulsed and squirmed as it drank blood and brain matter.

"All this to keep your boss distracted?" Crosby said. He turned the spotlight away from the giant potato having its meal. "I thought you were just going to kill two guys?"

"I need to keep my job," she said, walking around

the truck. "I can't have them trying to get Harv before me. I just need *time*. Time to set this all right again."

"So you plan to get away with that murder I just witnessed?"

Ramsey cut her eyes at him. "Don't start, Doug. This is good news. We're dealing with just one racist psychopath and not a brigade of 'em." She whistled and Spudley pulled its tentacle from Maxwell's face with a wet slurp. It waddled over to the truck and climbed into the bed, chattering nonsense. Ramsey and Crosby climbed into the cab. "Before you complain," she said, "remember that we've got five hours to go and your hands are still clean. Just think about all of Harv's money that you'll be getting."

Crosby gunned the engine and sped around the Dollar Store, heading for Harv Hallihan's place.

CHAPTER 14

SHE DIRECTED HIM to the dove field where she'd parked before. "There's a trail that cuts through his property," she said, lighting up her pipe. "I saw it when I came to kill him the first time. But we can't drive it. Gotta hike. Should only take an hour or so now that I know where we're going."

Ramsey put on her night vision goggles and started into the woods. The spud goblin ambled after her and Crosby followed. He kept his eyes trained on the monster and Ramsey equally. He knew they would both be more dangerous to him than Harv Hallihan or a Nazi biker. But there was the money to think of, and just like Ramsey, he could see a way for all of this chaos to work out in his favor in the end.

They found the trail and followed it deeper into the forest until they made it to the Hallihan farm. Ramsey stopped and steered them behind some bushes at the edge of the clearing. Ramsey and Crosby knelt on their knees and the spud goblin crouched between them. She took off her goggles and looked at the light coming from the barn. Crosby wiped the sweat from his face and whispered a question.

"Quiet," Ramsey said, lighting up her pipe and sucking hard.

"Jesus," Crosby said. "How much of that are you gonna use? You know it's affecting you."

Ramsey blew a thin stream of smoke into the bushes next to her. She let out a soft cough and said, "Makes sense that you wouldn't approve. But I got my reasons."

"Well, enlighten me," he hissed, "because I'm trespassing on some redneck maniac's property in the middle of the night next to a giant potato and a drug addict! I'm not saying any of this is your fault, Violet, but you just killed an officer of the law. What is your deal?"

Ramsey sniffled and rubbed her eyes. "My deal? Nobody knows my deal. Everybody thinks I'm GI Jane, but . . . "

She trailed off and Crosby knew that he'd reminded her of something bad. "I'm sorry, Violet," he said softly. "If you feel a little . . . well, damn near every veteran feels that way. I didn't see any combat but I know it's normal for it to fuck you up."

"I didn't see combat, either," she said.

"What? But everybody said . . . "

"That I'm a badass. That I was a warrior? A hero? I was over there for a week before I got taken out."

"What do you mean taken out?"

Ramsey took another hit from her pipe and blew out the smoke. "I was raped."

Even in the dark she could see Crosby's eyes widen.

"I got put in a squad and some of the roughnecks . . . they didn't like me. Barely got to know any of 'em before a bunch of 'em got me. I don't know why they did it but maybe it was 'cause I was good. Lotta boys in basic training hated how good I was. Would've only gotten worse in the arena. Everybody knew I was a good soldier, but over there . . . I think they wanted me to know that it didn't matter how good I was. They felt like things should be different for me over there. Harder. So they made it harder."

She rubbed at her eyes again. "Jesus," she whispered. "That's the most I've ever talked about it, right there."

"What happened?" he said.

She stared off at the barn. "Well . . . they drugged me. Don't remember much of it except, you know . . . the pain. I came to in the infirmary with my legs, ribs, and face all broken up. And I couldn't recall who it was exactly, but even if I could, I don't think they . . . "

"No," he said. "They wouldn't."

"Right. So I spent a week in bed, all by myself. Didn't even have any other patients in there. Like they didn't want me talking to anybody. They patched me up and sent me home and gave me a commendation, which . . . it was so vague that everybody just assumed I'd been blown up by an IED or something. Nobody asked and I didn't want to talk about it, so . . . "

She lit up her pipe again. Spudley purred softly at her.

"You know what?" she said. "I've been wanting to kill those fuckers ever since, whoever they are. Sometimes I can't help but think about how badly I want them dead. If I knew who they were I'd track 'em across the globe and snuff out their whole fuckin' families. And maybe it'd make me feel better, but I doubt it. Some shit you don't get better from."

Crosby felt like reaching across to touch her but knew it was a bad idea. Instead, he said, "Violet, I'm so sorry."

"Don't need your sorry," she said. "I've been managing just fine. I don't think I ever wanted to be a soldier anyway. Sounds stupid but I think I enlisted to be closer to my dad. But in the service . . . it's like anything else. It's organized as hell but really it's chaos. It's a sideshow that grinds people up, and that's not even considering that they're in the mass murder business. People get squashed underfoot, it's just how it is. Might as well be in prison. Or high school."

Then she burst into laughter, her mouth smiling wide and crooked. "I coulda been normal, once," she said through her ruined, toothless smile.

The rumble of an engine sounded in the woods behind them. A light came through the trees as the sound grew louder. Ramsey wiped her eyes and peered over the bushes to see a motorcycle ride out of the woods and down the trail toward the farm. "Okay," she whispered, putting away her pipe. "It's time."

Ramsey took Spudley's arm and wrapped it over her shoulder. The creature hopped onto her back like a child. She hiked out into the clearing, staying low, using the noise of the bike as cover. Crosby followed. They stopped by a patch of tall grass and ducked down to hide. The bike slowed and stopped and they watched Werewolf climb off his bike and head into the barn.

Ramsey turned to Crosby. "You stay at the door. We'll take care of the rest." Then she was off again, pulling out one of Crosby's Glocks and holding it in both hands. The potato clutched her back tightly, hopping up and down as she ran. Ramsey sneaked up to the dark side of the barn, then moved to the doorway and let Spudley off her back.

She darted inside and pointed the Glock, yelled "Freeze!"

Both men turned to look at her. Werewolf stood next to Harv's tractor, his entire head turning a furious crimson. Harv sat on a wooden stool at a table that stretched down the barn's wall. Ramsey noticed that while the barn appeared dilapidated from the outside, the interior had a polished concrete floor and every wall and ceiling joist was reinforced with new lumber. There were tables and barrels and a wide variety of scientific glassware, all meticulously organized. It was the neatest meth lab Ramsey had ever seen.

"You bitch," Werewolf growled.

"You're the ninja," Harv said calmly. "You came to kill me."

"That's right," said Ramsey. "Here to finish the job, includin' him." Her head gave a quick nod Werewolf.

As if on her signal, Spudley toddled in through the doorway. It raced around Ramsey on all fours, running straight for Werewolf. The biker managed to pull his gun and shoot the creature a few times as he charged him, but the bullets didn't slow it down. The goblin leapt up onto Werewolf and plunged its arms into his chest, the fibrous roots sliding in like oiled blades. Werewolf fell backward, his skull thudding against the concrete floor. His fingers twitched and his mouth stretched, trying to scream or gasp but only gurgling up gouts of blood. Spudley played in the hole it had dug, slapping at the blood and cutting fine trails through the canvas of Werewolf's ribcage. It slurped bright red meat with its spiky tentacles.

"Good boy," Ramsey said. The spud goblin looked

up from the shredded tatters of flesh that had been Werewolf. It was six feet tall now, the potato like a boulder, its eyes swaying in the air like ghost-white cobras.

Ramsey kept her gun trained on Harv, who watched the potato creature as it feasted on his partner. "You don't look like you'll miss him," she said.

Harv looked up at her. "He was racist scum."

"Why were you working for him, then?"

"I thought you didn't come here to ask me questions."

"Good point." Ramsey whistled and nodded again. The spud goblin moved away from the tractor and lumbered toward Harv. As it approached, it crouched onto its hands and feet, crawling slower, its eyestalks reaching out for him. It moved low to the ground until it was kneeling at Harv's feet. Harv reached down and petted the sprouts on top of Spudley's head. His fingers mingled with the roots without a scratch. The spud goblin's tentacle eyes reached up to caress its creator's fingertips.

"What the fuck is this?" Ramsey said.

"I've got no idea why it's doing this," Harv said.

"The fuck do you mean? You made it, didn't you?"

"Well, yes, but . . . you wouldn't understand. I designed their genetic structure, but this one has some kind of . . . personality. I didn't intend for that. Not sure I like it, either. I bred these things to be plants that behave like animals. This one's behaving like people. I wonder if the others will be the same. I wonder how big they'll get."

"Jesus, Harv . . . " said Ramsey. "Why did you make these for him?"

Harv waved his hand around and rolled his eyes. "Werewolf's real name was Richard, if you can believe that. He and all those White Dragons believed they were some kinda—what did they call it?—*racial revivalists*. Mostly they just wanted to hang out in their clubhouse and make money by transporting our drugs. But that wasn't good enough for Richard. He was the truest of true believers. So a while back, he started coming to me talking about biohazard weapons and asking what all I could do with genetics and biology. Then, one day, I hear he killed the leaders of his gang. Then he shows up and tells me I'll be making something new for him."

Ramsey gaped at him. "And you just *agreed to*?"

"He was gonna kill me, Deputy. Do I look much like a fighter?"

"What was he gonna do with 'em?"

"Bring down the entire American government, of course." Harv petted the spud goblin's brown skin. "Not that five hundred of these guys could wipe out the whole country. They'd probably just destroy a city or two. Werewolf had dreams of destroying modern society and all its modern weaknesses. He figured only the strongest deserved to prosper. How did he put it? Oh yeah, he'd be a 'primitivist warlord of a white tribal restoration.' He had an incredible vocabulary for a common thug, but I guess racist crackpots spend a lot of time explaining their beliefs. It's all they want to talk about, really."

"Why the fuck did you help him, Harv?" Ramsey shouted. "Look at what that thing can do! You were gonna help him spread it like a virus! *Why?*"

Harv waved his hand at the lab equipment spread across the wall-length table. "I've spread plenty of viruses in my time, Deputy. I don't do this work for a reason. I don't do it because I should or shouldn't. I just do it because *I can*."

"He's crazy," Crosby said.

Doug stood in the barn's doorway behind her, but Ramsey wouldn't take her eyes off Harv. "Right," she said. "Okay, Harv. We're shutting you down, and we want your cash. Tell us where it is and we won't cut your balls off with broken glass."

Harv shook his head like he was embarrassed for them.

Ramsey shot him in the knee.

Strangely, Harv barely moved. His kneecap had been obliterated and he only winced at the pain.

Spudley, however, roared. It reared up like a grizzly bear and stomped its tentacle feet. Its eyes waved hysterically at Ramsey as it turned its furious attention to her. She lowered her weapon as it plodded over. Spudley let out a deep groaning growl and slapped at the concrete in front of her.

Ramsey backed away. She figured that whatever reason Spudley had for not hurting her before, it had to be gone. Now that it had met its creator, it seemed like Ramsey meant nothing to it anymore. It could kill her now like anyone else. But, mere steps away from her, the creature flinched. Its eyestalks curled up and it retreated as red and blue lights flashed into the barn. A siren cut through the night as the sheriff's cruiser came down Harv's driveway.

CHAPTER 15

SPUDLEY COWERED FROM the strange noise and bright lights. Ramsey looked out of the barn's door and watched the cruiser pull up. Crosby was already walking out toward it, his hands over his head in surrender. Spudley grumbled next to the tractor, standing over the scattered remains of Werewolf. The giant potato fidgeted back and forth and picked at the corpse, sucking blood through its spiny fingers. Eating seemed to soothe it.

"I reckon this adventure of yours is over," Harv said.

Ramsey walked over to him and yanked him off his stool. Blood had poured down his pant leg from her previous shot. She held the Glock against his cheek and said, "It's not over until I burn this farm to the ground."

They waited a few moments, watching the spinning police lights flashing through the barn door. Ramsey heard voices outside.

"Violet!" Crosby called from outside. "I told them everything. It's over. I know you want to keep your job . . . but this is bigger than that. Those things still have to be destroyed!" He probably thought he could negotiate with Sheriff Ruth. The idiot.

Ramsey closed her eyes. "Come in here and say it!" she said.

In a few moments Crosby was in the doorway again. Just behind him were LaGrange and Sheriff Ruth, their guns drawn.

"The fuck is that thing?" LaGrange shouted, pointing his gun over at Spudley.

"That's the cause of all this," Ramsey said.

Sheriff Ruth hadn't taken his eyes off Ramsey and Harv. "Did you do that?" he asked, nodding at Harv's knee.

"'Bout to do worse, boss," Ramsey said.

"You need help, Violet," said Crosby.

"Shut the fuck up, Doug," she said. "You're not helping."

"I think Doug's right," said the sheriff. "You need help."

"First person to try anything is gonna have that giant tater eating their face. See if it doesn't."

Sheriff Ruth took a step forward. "Then how you gonna play this, Deputy? You gonna murder Harv right in front of us? You know we'd have to kill you. What's he done to you anyway?"

"He's gotta die," Ramsey said. "This whole farm's gotta come down. I understand why you wouldn't want that to happen, Sheriff. I've never got in your way before. Don't get in my way now. Just take Doug back to his home and let me finish this. We can all go home and get on with our lives."

Sheriff Ruth gave some thought to her proposal, then finally lowered his eyes. He looked over to LaGrange and nodded. LaGrange brought the butt of his pistol down on the back of Crosby's head. Crosby fell to his knees, and as he reached for his wound

LaGrange took his wrist and twisted it up behind his back. He poked his gun into Crosby's neck and sneered with sadistic pleasure.

"Let him go, Violet," Willis said. He took another step toward Ramsey, who moved backward, dragging Harv with her.

"Look at that thing!" Ramsey yelled, pointing at Spudley. "He's made hundreds of 'em! He was gonna let that psycho turn 'em loose and kill thousands of people! You're just gonna let him get away with it?"

"I didn't know anything about it, Violet," said Sheriff Ruth. "You know that. Just let him go and I'll deal with him."

"Fuck you, old man. I'm the one who tracked all this down to him. I'm the one who did the police work. I've always done the work while you pretend you're the one running shit. You're nothin' but a two-bit hustler. You're a small-town lackey for dipshit bikers. That's all you ever were. But you probably don't care, do you? Just like Harv here."

The sheriff spoke in a calm monotone. "Let him go," he repeated, "or we take care of your friend here. Please . . . just do as I say, girl . . . or he's a dead man."

Ramsey looked at Crosby, on his knees, wincing in pain, LaGrange's gun at his throat.

"Fuck 'im," she said.

Crosby's eyes shot open. "What?"

"You're gonna let an innocent man die?" Willis asked. "You ain't got it in you, girl."

"You don't fuckin' know me, Willis."

"He's got a decent life he's made. He's got a family. He's got much more to live for than you do."

"Fuck his life," she said. "Fuck his wife. Fuck all his kids. I don't give a shit. You're not callin' the shots here, Willis." For a moment, she saw it in the sheriff's eyes, a bubbling indignant rage that made his teeth start to grind. It looked like he was going to call her a bitch.

He shot her instead.

Willis was a fast draw, and accurate as hell. His bullet missed Harv's head and slammed square into Ramsey's chest. She fell back, her lungs shocked into paralysis. Harv came down right next to her.

At the gunshot, the spud goblin roared and beat the floor with its spiky fists. It charged at the three men in the barn's doorway. LaGrange pushed Crosby away and started firing. He emptied his gun into Spudley's massive body, which absorbed every bullet. With a swing of its arm it cleaved LaGrange's head from his body. Blood shot up from the deputy's carotid artery and splashed a ceiling joist overhead.

Willis Ruth was already shooting, hitting Spudley in its eye stalks. The potato creature roared in pain and covered its face with its tentacles. The sheriff reloaded his pistol with an extended clip and kept firing, filling Spudley's body with hollow point bullets that tore away its brown papery skin and sent chunks of wet potato meat flying.

The spud goblin groaned in pain and its limbs twitched at its sides. It fell to its knees as Sheriff Ruth loaded another clip and kept blasting away until the creature's face disintegrated and its body slumped down against the concrete. A puddle of mashed goop spread out from its shredded body. Sheriff Willis Ruth, with flecks of blood and gobs of white potato on his face, walked over and kicked at Harv's body. He didn't move, but Ramsey did. Her lower lip twitched, struggling to draw breath again and producing only a weak whisper. Through blurred vision and watery eyes, she could see Sheriff Ruth standing over her like a titan, pointing his gun down at her like God's own vengeance.

He fell to the floor.

She saw Crosby in his blue Braves hoodie, holding a shovel.

Then he was helping her up. Ramsey's hand quivered and her arm was numb, but she managed to reach between the buttons of her shirt and pull at the Velcro on her bulletproof vest.

Crosby sat her on the stool at the worktable and helped her out of the vest. Beneath it, she wore a tank top stained with sweat. Ramsey took rapid, shallow breaths. She looked up at Crosby, sure that she should apologize to him, but then saw Sheriff Ruth stirring on the ground next to Harv.

She pushed Crosby away and snatched the shovel from him. She got up from the stool and closed in on the sheriff. Ramsey wanted to say something to him. To tell him that there was a price for his type of arrogance. That he just another hillbilly in the middle of nowhere, and that all this happened because he let his little backwoods gang get out of his own control. She wanted to say it, but she only had enough breath in her to beat him to death with the shovel.

CHAPTER 16

THEY FOUND A lockbox underneath Harv's worktable and the key on a pegboard. Crosby unloaded stacks and stacks of cash into a potato sack, and when Ramsey wasn't looking he took the sack and left the barn, walking off into the woods for his truck.

In truth, she saw him. She just didn't stop him.

Ramsey looked over the crime scene. Willis Ruth lay dead with his face caved in, LaGrange was decapitated, and Werewolf was just a red stain smeared across the floor. Spudley had been reduced to a hill of potato chunks. Ramsey looked out the back door of the barn to the fields. Hundreds of tiny spud goblins wiggled in the soil, their heads poking out into the night air. Every one of them rotated inside their holes like prairie dogs, turning to stare at her with little white root balls for eyes.

Something stirred behind her, and she turned to see Harv Hallihan trying to pull himself across the floor. "Don't bother," Ramsey told him. "You've lost too much blood."

Harv grumbled. "Shit. This is where my big brain gets me. Same stupid death as anybody else."

Ramsey leaned over the man and looked into his face. He was pale, sheened with sweat, but composed.

"And here I am," she said. "Too tired to kill you. Lay there and die, Harv. Or try and stop me. I don't care."

"What're you gonna . . . "

"I'm gonna take care of those poisonous little lifeforms you made. A woman cleaning up your mess, Harv. That's all this is."

Ramsey fired up Harv's tractor and rode out into the field. She followed the lines he'd plowed, only she made sure the tires rode over the potatoes instead of between them. She crushed them under the tractor's weight, puttering around the field in circles until each little sprout had been smooshed open, exposing their white meat to the open air. The creatures groaned and screamed in their gurgling high-pitched voices as she killed them. Ramsey smoked her pipe, obsessing over the destruction of each and every one of them.

She parked the tractor back in the barn without shutting off the engine. She rifled through some of Harv's things before finding a can of diesel fuel. She splashed it all over the barn, covering Harv's meth assembly line, then the bodies, then the tractor. Harv watched her from his place on the floor, his breath coming in weak little gasps. She gave him a splash of fuel and dropped a match as she left.

The whole barn went up in flames. She didn't hear Harv make a single sound as he burned alive. When the inferno was raging into the night air, Ramsey rode away on Werewolf's motorcycle.

She raced down the trail through Harv's property and came out on the highway. The wind whirled her loose hair and the first splinters of dawn shined through the strands. She rode to the Dollar Store, which was still closed, and laid the bike down next to Maxwell's mostly headless body. She started hiking across town, trying to walk steadily, like she hadn't been up for a day smoking meth and exterminating mutant potatoes and burning people to death.

A firetruck blasted down the highway as she got to the Waffle House where she'd parked her Blazer.

CHAPTER 17

WILLIS RUTH'S DEATH started a firestorm in the media that almost swallowed Whaley County whole. The FBI were investigating anything Willis or Harv ever did. They cordoned off Harv's property and cleaned out Willis' office. They pored over his records, which was easy since Willis was so organized, and when they had pretty much everything locked down, it was time to interview Violet Ramsey, the last one standing.

They asked her about drug running and money laundering, extortion and threats. They asked her about LaGrange's assault charges and Maxwell's debts to a casino across the state line. They asked about Harv Hallihan and the White Dragon Motorcycle Club. Ramsey explained that she had her suspicions about Sheriff Ruth, and she'd heard rumors about him like everyone else had, but she knew nothing about his activities or associates. She told them that Sheriff Ruth likely kept her around because of her reputation. To give the department a sense of legitimacy while they committed their crimes. "And I went along with it," she said, "because I need this job. I'm pretty much alone in the world."

They appointed an interim sheriff, an old college

campus cop named Tommy Tracy. He and Ramsey got along well enough, and he didn't pry into her life, which she thanked him for. Sheriff Tracy would only hold the position until the next election. In her last follow-up interview with the state investigators, they told her they were signing over Willis' orange Charger to her, as compensation for the embarrassment she'd suffered as part of his department. They suggested that she run for sheriff herself.

That's when she knew she'd gotten away with everything.

CHAPTER 18

CROSBY HID THE cash in his storage shed and told himself he wouldn't touch it for ten years.

But the money wasn't all he'd taken from Harv Hallihan's place. He'd taken a piece of Spudley, too. Crosby kept the little chunk of potato in a glass jar, and over the next few weeks the little chunk began to grow white roots as fine as hairs. Then the tiny tendrils spread along the interior of the glass and the potato meat in the center pulsed as if it were breathing.

Crosby drove into the city on a Monday afternoon to meet with a biology professor at the University. He wanted to get a professional opinion. This thing that Harv had created was one of a kind. Crosby figured there were hundreds of scientific applications it could be used for. Whether it cured something or caused something worse, it was worth money. He sat on a bench in the lobby of the science building, staring at a glass case full of cat skeletons and waiting for his appointment.

Then a woman in a brown uniform walked in. Crosby didn't look up as she took a seat on the opposite side of the bench. "Hello, Violet," he said.

"What are you doing here, Doug?"

"My business."

"You have a piece of it, don't you?"

He glanced around the lobby. No one was close enough to hear them and the professor still hadn't come down the stairs.

"Listen here," she said under her breath. "That thing's too dangerous to live, so you're not gonna show it to anybody. You're gonna give it to me so I can take care of it."

"I'm not trying to—"

"Oh, I don't care what your reasons are, Doug. Hell, you could just be fascinated by it like Harv was. You could also be a tenth degree black belt . . . and I'd still beat your ass right here in this room and take it from you. So . . . ?"

Crosby took out the jar and placed it on the bench between them. Ramsey snatched it up and held it on her lap.

"Thank you, Doug. Is this all there is? Do you have any of it at your home?"

"No," he said.

"Be honest, now. You don't want that thing around your family."

"Jesus, Violet, calm down. This isn't a Jason Statham movie."

"I'm just covering my bases."

"Like you care about my family anyway? I distinctly remember you saying that you didn't give a shit about us."

"That's right," Ramsey said. "And it's funny you mention that because that brings me to my next point. First, I want to say that I don't want to do anything rash. But I told you things that night that nobody else knows, and . . . and I can't let you share that information. Especially not your wife and kids, who are the first ones you'd tell. So you need to forget what you know about me . . . that way I won't have to firebomb your house."

Doug Crosby's eyes went cold. "Bitch, if you ever—"

"I know, I know, I expected that reaction, Doug. But, like I said, I'm just covering my bases. I'm threatenin' you now with words so I don't have to do it later with actions. If you act like a gentleman and keep your mouth shut about me for the rest of your life, it'll never have to matter. So now that we understand each other, how about we both head back home?"

Crosby got to his feet. He started for the door, and as he passed he said, "You're crazy, Violet."

She wanted to smirk at him and say something cool. To tell him to get his ass back to Whaley County before she whupped him in front of all these fancy college kids.

But she didn't say anything.

She sat on the bench, alone, and watched him walk away.

CHAPTER 19

RAMSEY RETURNED HOME that afternoon.

With most of her furniture destroyed, the trailer was almost empty. The holes in her black walls had been patched with white drywall mud. The carpet still needed to be shampooed. Her mother had been devastated that someone broke in and wrecked the place, but mostly because she was worried about Violet's safety. She insisted on driving out to visit but Ramsey spent an hour assuring her mother that the perpetrator was some random tweaker who just wanted to pawn her guns for drugs. Her mother accepted the story. Ramsey's sanctuary was hers once again.

After she removed her uniform, Ramsey went out to her garden and dug in the dirt. She sat the glass jar with the potato chunk on the ground next to her. She thought about Spudley, how it had been so much like a child. She wondered if that made her the thing's mother. Or if Harv was its father. She wondered if the little chunk in the jar could grow into another Spudley. Maybe it would remember the taste of her blood and continue to be her friend. She wondered how big it would get over time, how dangerous and destructive it would become if it was allowed to be free.

She never considered planting it to find out.

Instead, she dumped the potato piece onto her hibachi grill and soaked it in gasoline. She lit a match and watched the chunk pulse in the orange flames, its tendrils writhing in pain. Slowly, its body melted into a greasy ooze that dripped from the grill's metal bars. When it was nothing but ashes, she went back to her garden.

As she planted her new flowers and peppers, Ramsey looked up at the little shed she'd built on the other side of the x-shaped garden. Using some of the equipment she'd scavenged from Harv, she'd put together a modest laboratory. The first batch she'd made wasn't near the quality she used to get from Bugs, but in time she'd make better stuff. She'd already made a ritual of it.

THE END

ABOUT THE AUTHOR

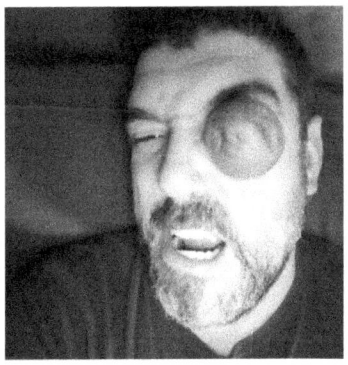

David W Barbee writes weird stories full of dark monsters and strange maniacs, influenced by a deranged childhood diet of cartoons, comic books, and cult movies. *Taterskinheads* is his sixth book.

All Art is Junk by R. A. Harris

Lana Rivers, a girl with paintbrush hair, is missing and it's up to Lancelot, her cyborg knight, and his bionic conjoined twin, Cilia, to find her before her evil father, a disrespected artist turned mad-scientist, performs a terrible experiment on her.

Cherub by David C. Hayes

Cherub wasn't like the other boys—too slow, too rough—but he didn't deserve what that hospital did to him, and now he will make them pay.

Skinners by Adam Millard

Los Angeles, the City of Angels. At least, that's what the brochure says. What it fails to mention is the earthquakes. Oh, and the flesh-eating creatures lying dormant beneath the concrete, waiting for the chance to surface once again. Their wait is over . . .

The After-Life Story of Pork Knuckles Malone by MP Johnson

What's a farm boy to do when his pet pig becomes an evil, decaying hunk of ham with slime-spewing psychic powers?

A Lightbulb's Lament by Grant Wamack

A gentleman with a lightbulb for head wakes up in a world full of darkness, hooks up with a beautiful ex-prostitute, and an old man who can heal people; he travels down south to find the mysterious Creator.

PseudoPsalms by Peter Adam Saloman

Bram Stoker nominated author Peter Adam Salomon has laid bare the intricate horrors of the human condition in this poetic compilation; PseudoPsalms: Saints v. Sinners.

Gravity Comics Massacre by Vincenzo Bilof

An absolutely shitty novella involving comic books, aliens, a serial killer, teenagers in an abandoned town, horror-trope dream sequences, and an ending you're going to hate.

Glue by Scott Lange

Sticky bowels and sticky situations.

Ascent by Matthew Bialer

Is the 8 foot tall creature haunting a small town in Iowa in the fall of the year 1903 the product of a hoax and collective imagination or was it one of the first documented paranormal event in America? This epic poem grapples with these questions.

Fecal Terror by David Bernstein

A killer turd is on the loose!

The Fairy Princess of Trains
by Christopher Boyle

Danny's mediocre life turns upside-down when his couch starts whispering to him. Then he's charged with a supernatural mission: Rescue the Fairy Princess of Trains.

Terence, Mephisto & Viscera Eyes
by Chris Kelso

9 new science fiction stories from Chris Kelso

Bizarro Bizarro: An Anthology

The finest bizarro short stories from 2013.

Notes from the Guts of a Hippo
by Grant Wamack

A rugged journalist travels to Brazil in search of a missing hippo researcher and the notes left behind lead to something earth shatteringly revelatory.

Day of the Milkman by S. T. Cartledge

In a world dominated by the milk industry, only one milkman survives after a terrible storm sinks all the ships and throws the Great White Sea out of balance.

Moosejaw Frontier by Chris Kelso

An unapologetic disaster of metafiction

Notes from the Guts of a Hippo
by Grant Wamack

A rugged journalist travels to Brazil in search of a missing hippo researcher and the notes left behind lead to something earth shatteringly revelatory.

Industrial Carpet Drag by Bruce Taylor

Chemicals make you do great things!

Necrosaurus Rex by Nicolas Day

Necrosaurus Rex tells the tale of Martin, a simple janitor, who takes an unfortunate trip through time, becomes a violent mutant, and the father of us all. There's 14 billion years crushed inside these pages, and most of them are pretty nasty.

The Boy Who Loved Death by Hal Duncan

From blackest humour to bleakest horror, with twisted relish, Hal Duncan's eighteen tales dig into death—and the life that goes with it.

X's for Eyes by Laird Barron

Between the machinations of the disciples of black gods and good old corporate skullduggery, it's winding up to be of a hell of a summer vacation for the Tooms Brothers.

Omega Grey by Seb Doubinsky

When professor Todd Bailer embarked on a psychedelics quest to discover if the land of the Dead really existed, he had no idea he would threaten the cosmic balance of the universe by triggering a real-estate conquest of the new Frontier.

Berzerkoids by MP Johnson

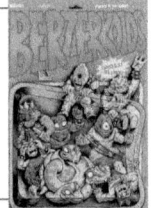

The first short story collection from Wonderland Book Award-winning author MP Johnson

Elusive Plato by Rhys Hughes

The last in a long decadent line of piratical Spanish eccentrics, Bartleby Cadiz grows up in isolation to be as mad, bad and metaphysical as his ancestors. But he feels there is something different about him. What can it be?

Boiled
Americans
Michael Allen Rose

Boiled Americans
by Michael Allen Rose

Boiled Americans is a puzzle box in book form, inspired by the violence of living in urban America and exploding the tendency to forget or ignore.

Great American Slasher
by David C. Hayes

Baseball, apple pie . . . and murder.

The Bohemian Guide to Monogamy
by Andrew Armacost

Here, a strange labyrinth of interlinked short fiction assembles itself into a darkly moving novella that deftly explores the bottomless pain and pleasure of love and commitment.

Surreal Worlds edited by Sean Leonard

An anthology of surrealistic compositions created by some of the finest names in genre fiction. A showcase of international talent undaunted by the conventions of language and common narrative structures. Here is timelessness. Here is Surreal Worlds

How to Succesfully Kidnap Strangers
by Max Booth III

Do not respond to bad reviews. If you must respond to bad reviews, please do not kidnap the reviewer.

ADHD Vampire by Matthew Vaughn

He came, he conquered, he was distracted a lot

Static/Orgone by Jamie Grefe

A double-novella of literary grindhouse nightmares and theoretical post-apocalyptic vengeance.

Retch by David Bernstein

What would you do if you were cursed to puke right before you reached orgasm? You'd do anything, right? (You know you would.) Find out what one wealthy, good-looking, playboy will do to try to end his abhorrent curse.

Battering the Stem by Bob Freville

A darkly comic urban crime novella. What would it take to make you beg?

Wonder Weavers by Matthew Bialer

An epic poem about a mysterious sighting in 1896.

Cartoons in the Suicide Forest by Leza Cantoral

When we're dead
You know she'll adore us

www.ingramcontent.com/pod-product-compliance
Lightning Source LLC
Chambersburg PA
CBHW072150190626
46811CB00018B/3055